"I want revenge. On [...] friend Mace, and for . . . well, everything. I want to see justice done." Kerry steeled herself. "I didn't know myself why I wanted so badly to find you, but now I do. What I want is for you to help me . . . to teach me. To make me powerful enough to fight her."

Mother Blessing laughed suddenly, little bits of Oreo spraying the varnished wood tabletop. "Child," she said finally. "Y'all are a spirited one, aren't you?"

Now that she had declared her purpose, Kerry saw no reason to back down. "I'm sorry," she said, "but I am completely serious. Daniel said the craft could be learned, that one didn't have to be born a witch."

"Daniel was right," Mother Blessing agreed. "But even so, I don't know you myself. How do I know if I can trust y'all with the kind of power you're talkin' about, the kind that could make y'all a challenge to Season? How do I even know you haven't joined up with her?"

Kerry felt her face flush with anger. "I wouldn't!" she raged. "She killed the man I love."

As the seasons change, so does Kerry. . . .
Check out the other installments
in the Witch Season series:

Summer

And coming soon from Simon Pulse:

Winter

Spring

witch
season

FALL

JEFF MARIOTTE

Simon Pulse
New York London Toronto Sydney

For Maryelizabeth, who enchanted me a long time ago.

SIMON PULSE
An imprint of Simon & Schuster
Children's Publishing Division
1230 Avenue of the Americas, New York, NY 10020

Copyright © 2004 by Jeff Mariotte
All rights reserved, including the right of
reproduction in whole or in part in any form.

SIMON PULSE and colophon are
registered trademarks of Simon & Schuster, Inc.

Designed by Ann Zeak
The text of this book was set in Bembo.

Manufactured in place the United States of America
First Simon Pulse edition October 2004
10 9 8 7 6 5 4 3 2 1

Library of Congress Control Number 2004103416

ISBN 0-689-86724-7

Thanks to Michelle Nagler, who had to come in late, Amanda Berger, Bethany Buck, Howard and Mara, and a bunch of people who provide all kinds of support, including but not limited to Tara, Cindy, Cari, Chris, John, Jack, and the rest of you.

Kerry Profitt's diary, October 14.

So, okay, college? Not exactly what I figured it'd be.

I mean, the campus is nice, the classes moderately interesting. My favorite is an American history lecture from one Dr. Page Manning, who is not only a terrific and often funny speaker, but can really make the subject come alive.

Not in the way that Daniel Blessing could, of course. But then, Daniel lived a lot more of it. I think it is his influence, though, that inspired me to take the class in the first place, letting me see history in a way that I never had, as something more than just dates and battles and the names of dead white men. I'm thinking about it as a major.

Minoring in depression, I guess.

I miss him SO much. Like I said, college is okay, but it's full of skimpy outfitted Britneys and baggy-pantsed, backward-hat boys trying to grow goatees and personalities at the same time, and after what I went through this summer, what WE went through, Scott and Brandy and Rebecca and Josh and poor Mace, and me—and Daniel, who, like Mace, paid the ultimate price—sitting in lecture halls, taking notes, doing homework in the dorm . . . it all just seems so tame. So removed from the rest of the world.

Not that I'd know what the rest of the world was really like, having spent most of my life removed from it by one thing or another. But still, you know.

It's like the summer was in Technicolor and campus life is in sepia tones. Washed out sepia, at that. I keep finding my mind flashing back to San Diego, to the hunt for Season Howe that consumed us all. And to the final battle that Daniel didn't survive.

I don't know where Season is now, obviously. I couldn't fight her if I did. But I feel like if I saw her today, I'd rip her apart with my bare hands, so pumped up with righteous wrath that she couldn't begin to hold me back.

The nightmares haven't come back, so that's one small blessing (a word I have to remember not to capitalize, or to precede with "Daniel" on certain occasions). But my waking thoughts are so dark, so violent, sometimes so hopeless, that it's hard to see the difference.

No, I take that back. I never really knew where the nightmares came from. I know perfectly well where this darkness originates, though. It comes from having watched the man I love get killed.

Murdered, right in front of me, by an evil witch named Season Howe.

And some day, some how, she's going to pay.

More later,

K.

1

"Kerry?"

Kerry Profitt tore her gaze away from the screen of her laptop. She had lost focus anyway, the words she'd been typing blurred behind a film of tears. "Yeah?"

Sonya, her roommate in Northwestern University's Elder Hall, looked at her from her own desk with motherly concern. Sonya's eyes were big and brown, accentuated all the more by small-lensed but thick glasses and an expression of perpetual curiosity, as if she were a visitor to this world, trying to take in everything at a single glance. Sonya tugged a lock of her short, dark hair away from her cheek and positioned it behind her ear. "You okay?" she asked.

"Yeah, I'm . . . you know. Fine."

"Because you don't look so okay," Sonya

went on. "What with the tears kind of splashing on your keyboard, I thought maybe there was something bothering you."

"Well, I guess maybe a little," Kerry admitted. She hadn't given Sonya the What-I-Did-On-My-Summer-Vacation talk, not expecting that her roommate, or, when it came right down to it, anyone else, would believe a word of it. And maybe it'd be worse if they did believe it, because she knew how hard it was to deal with the fact that the world was so much different than she had thought it was. Things she had always believed to be unreal, to be fantasy, had turned out to be absolutely true. It made "real" life seem like a cartoon, like someone else's version of reality. Why force that knowledge onto others?

She had, to cover her sometimes abrupt moments of grieving, told Sonya about the deaths of her parents, and said that they had been topped off by the death of a boyfriend over the summer. She just avoided the minor details, such as precisely how the boyfriend had died, and the fact that he had been a very powerful witch who was almost three hundred years old.

"Daniel?" Sonya asked.

Kerry nodded. "I miss him. A whole lot."

Sonya turned in her chair, and Kerry thought she was about to give her the You've-Got-To-Move-On-With-Your-Life lecture again. But Sonya was wise enough to catch the way that Kerry tensed—a pose that said, *If you start that again I* will *pummel you*—and she restrained herself. "I'm going out with Dougie and Ben," she said instead, naming the two guys she was juggling, though it seemed that Dougie was winning out. "Maybe get some falafel, have a beer. You want to come?"

Kerry appreciated the invitation, and said so. "But I'll stay in," she added. "I still have a bunch of homework to get done before tomorrow."

Sonya shrugged. "As long as you're really doing homework," she said, "and not sitting here by yourself *pining*."

"No," Kerry tried to assure her. "I'm okay, really."

The truth was she didn't want to have falafel and beer with Dougie and Ben and Sonya. Their interests were not hers, their lives seemed flat and boring somehow. They would talk about professors and classmates, or the latest band that had captured their fancy, or they'd dis some style they hadn't taken up yet but would soon. She'd been part of such conversations in the past, and probably would be again—she remembered, with some fondness, how all she'd wanted at the beginning of the summer was to have a "normal" life, like everyone else's. Now she had an opportunity to have just that, and it couldn't have held less interest for her.

"You say so." Sonya gave her short hair a little flip, pulled a jacket off a hook by the door, and left.

The room, with Sonya out of it, suddenly felt twice its real size. She was a perfectly nice girl, but her presence in the room seemed to suck the air out of it. Kerry knew it was her own fault, not Sonya's—anyone else would be glad to have Sonya for a roommate. *I'm spoiled,* she thought, *that's what it is. I want Daniel, or nothing at all.*

She wondered if it was stupid to spend her life wishing for things she couldn't have. It probably was, she decided—a huge waste of time and energy. Trouble was, she didn't know quite what she could do about it. She was who she was, and if there was a way to change that she didn't know it.

She went to the window and looked at the campus spread out below her third-floor window. Trees flamed yellow and red in the glow cast by streetlights and spilling from the dorm. The Illinois air was crisp but not yet cold—jackets were required at night, but the days were still warm enough for shirts and the occasional sweater. She had always liked this time of year, before—the cool evenings, the back-to-school excitement, then the Halloween season that led to football games and Thanksgiving and Christmas. Even now she could feel herself wanting to be caught up in it.

But if you have to want it, she thought sadly, *it's not really happening, is it? More wishing, that's all. I wish I didn't wish so much.*

Rebecca Levine soaked in the big clawfooted bathtub of the house she and her friend Erin had rented near downtown Santa Cruz before summer break started. It wasn't much of a house—a run-down Victorian with faded green paint, floorboards that creaked like something from a horror movie, and wiring she was convinced would someday burn the whole thing to the ground. But they had a cat, and the plumbing worked fine and the water in the tub was steaming hot, and she had placed scented candles around the room before she got in. At some point Erin would yell at her to get out because they only had the one bathroom, but until that happened she'd make the most of it.

She had always loved baths, but during the last month of summer she hadn't had much opportunity to indulge. Too much had been going on—and it had been so sad. Now that it was all over, at least for her, she was trying to make up for August's privation. It had taken her a couple of weeks just to relax enough to do it, not to jump every time there was an unexpected noise or a shadow fell across her path. She still wasn't back to what she considered routine, and didn't know if she ever would be. But she was determined not to let that prevent her from indulging herself whenever she could.

Sleep? That was hard to come by, at least sleep uninterrupted by horrible visions and memories of Mace and Daniel and Season Howe. But in here, wet and steamy and alone, she could relax, let her mind float to happy places. Private sandy beaches, mountains thrusting up from canopied jungles, sidewalk cafés on wide Parisian boulevards . . . these were comforting images for Rebecca, and comfort was what she needed most. Holding Reynolds, their mutt of an alley cat, and feeling the motor of his purr while she read helped too. She'd gained almost ten pounds in the last couple of weeks, thanks to the comfort foods she had allowed herself. While she had never been skinny or cared that she wasn't, she recognized that eating her way to sanity was never going to work. So, the baths, the pampering, the self-indulgence.

Her classes this semester were pretty cool, though she was having a hard time getting into them. She was taking a poli sci class focusing on twentieth-century American political history, an introductory psych class, and an entomology class, figuring that the only way to get over a lifelong fear of bugs was to learn more about them. No luck on that, so far. Actually, knowing what insects could do to people only beefed up that particular phobia. At the same time, though, being afraid of creepy-crawlies at least took some of the edge off being afraid that Season Howe might come around at any time.

Rebecca breathed deeply, inhaling the aroma of the lilac-scented bath water and the vanilla candle nearest the tub. She luxuriated in the tactile sensation of the hot water against her skin and tried to push aside all other thoughts and cares.

If only she didn't ever have to come out . . .

"Pop Tart?"

"Eeew," Brandy said, just as Scott had known she would. "How can you put that stuff in your body?"

He took a bite and spoke with his mouth full, letting crumbs spill out over his lips. "Kind of like this," he said, facing her and enjoying the way her pretty face twisted in revulsion. This one was strawberry, and fresh from the toaster so the filling was especially soft and gooey. She waved him away from her with an urgent motion.

"Yuck! Go away!"

Instead, he lowered his head toward hers, crumbs dropping onto the chemistry text spread in front of her on their dining room table. "Kiss me, baby," he demanded around the mouthful. "Gimme some sugar."

Now Brandy physically pushed him away, her hand against his shoulder. "All the sugar you're getting is already in your mouth," she told him.

Scott decided the joke had gone far enough and he turned away, finishing the bite in a more mannerly fashion. He loved to gross her out because she was such an easy target, but he knew that her tolerance for it was very limited, and on those occasions when he'd pushed too much her reaction had changed from good-humored to genuinely furious without notice. And a furious Brandy Pearson was a sight that Scott Banner didn't want to see too many times in his life.

"Sorry, babe," he said after he'd swallowed and chased the mouthful with a drink of water.

"Sure you are." Her words were clipped, her tone honestly angry. If he hadn't gone over the edge he'd come close to it, that was for sure.

"I'm just teasing, you know that."

"That kind of teasing I can do without."

Brandy had changed, Scott thought, since the summer. Her sense of humor—never her strongest suit to begin with—had diminished somehow, as if life just wasn't as funny as it had once been. He liked it when she laughed, loved the contrast between her even white teeth and her dark face, but these days it happened less and less. Although she had thrown herself into her studies at Harvard, she didn't seem any more removed from him—they held hands as they walked across campus just as they'd done before, they made love from time to time, they kissed when they parted and when they reunited. But the not-laughing thing bothered him, more than he wanted to admit even to himself.

He touched her shoulder gently. "I know. I'm sorry," he said again. He hoped he sounded sincere. The other thing about Brandy—*okay,* he realized, *this has always been true, but more so since the summer*—was that he really hated to be on her bad side. Not just because he loved her and wanted to make her happy, but because she was a little scary when she was angry. He'd seen the power of rage now—Season Howe had demonstrated that—and Brandy was nowhere near that kind of level. But still, Scott guessed, he was a little gun-shy.

"Just . . . try to be an adult," she admonished him. "Pretend, anyway."

The rest of their apartment was dark, the only lights burning the ones in the dining area, where they did most of their studying. The table was almost lost under mounds of books and papers, with precious little space left for actual dining. A living room opened onto the dining area, with a computer, TV, and stereo system, and past that their cramped bedroom waited. Scott knew that he needed to put some space between them right now—space and time. If he turned on the TV or music, though, she'd complain that it was interfering with her studying. Instead, he grabbed a short-story anthology off one of the stacks on the table. "I'm going to read for a while," he said, and headed toward the bedroom, where he could find solitude and solace until she decided to join him.

Space. And time.

UNLV would have usurped all of Josh Quinn's time if he'd let it, but the casinos beckoned, and he couldn't bring himself to ignore their call. Every time he saw them, neon shining so bright that the stars dimmed, he felt like Ulysses tied to the mast, trying to resist the sirens.

But there was no one to bind Josh down, and Ulysses hadn't fared all that well either, come to think of it. So whenever he didn't need to be in class—and sometimes when he did—Josh found himself haunting the Strip or the older casinos downtown. *Ocean's 11* country— the original, not the lame remake. On this night, that's where he was, downtown at the Golden Nugget, enveloped in a soundtrack of bells and buzzers and clanging coins. He was too young to gamble by a few years but he had a fake ID that no one ever checked. He didn't have much money to risk at the best of times, and this was not the best of times, so he resigned himself to video poker. It was hard to win big at that, but it was possible to play for a long time on a ten-dollar roll of quarters.

He'd been sitting at the machine for almost forty minutes, puffing on a succession of smokes, feeding the coins in one or two at a time, playing his hands with as much care as he could, considering the machine was also the dealer. He punched the deal button and was dealt two fives—hearts and clubs—the jack of spades, ten of hearts, and seven of diamonds. A nothing hand, pretty much, and he'd blown two quarters on it. Two hearts . . . he could shoot for a flush but that was almost a guaranteed loser. He had a pair, but that wouldn't net him much. Keep the jack and dump the rest?

Finally he kept the two fives, pathetic as they were, and drew three new cards. Nine of spades and two eights. Now with two pair, the machine paid off. Still small change, but it would keep him going for a while.

If he ran out of money then he'd have to start the long walk back home. And if he did that, walking through the shadowed streets away from the lights and the action, then he'd think about her. About Season, and how she'd ripped the life from Daniel Blessing.

He didn't want to think about that. Instead, he fed two more quarters into the slot.

2

Home again, after far too long. The journey was an arduous one, as I had been in San Francisco when I received Mother Blessing's urgent summons. Urgent or no, one can only cross this great nation at a certain speed, even by railroad. Arriving at Norfolk, I hired a carriage and drove to the old Slocumb site, where she keeps a skiff for precisely such visits.

Great Dismal Swamp greeted me as it always does, and this was my first real indication that I had indeed come home. The smells of the brackish water and the white-cedar, the screams and cries of blackbirds, warblers, and robins, the mechanical knocking of woodpeckers, the incessant drone of mosquitoes: All these things brought a rush *of memory to my mind, memories of my youth growing up among these marshes and bogs, learning the craft at Mother Blessing's side. No matter where I travel—to the jagged peaks of the Rocky Mountains, the softly sculpted dunes of Arabia, the villages of Europe—Great Dismal's walls of trees and thick cover of ferns, mosses, camellia, and dwarf trillium remain the standard of natural beauty in my heart.*

As I poled the skiff through the swamp, I watched for the long-missed but always-remembered landmarks—the lightning-split oak, the stand of baldcypress shaped like the corner of a log fort, the trio of stumps rumored to have been cut by George Washington himself, rising up from the water like swimmers seeking air—that would presently lead me to Mother Blessing's cabin.

Soon enough, I was here, and that is when I learned the reason for her call. Mother Blessing lay atop her bed, flushed and fevered, writhing and thrashing in evident pain. I quickly performed a healing spell, glad that even through her delirium, she had been able to reach out to me in time.

My spell calmed her and broke her fever, and before long she was sleeping soundly.

While waiting for her to recover, I cleaned the cabin, which had been clearly suffering from neglect due to her illness. By evening she was awake and alert enough to drink some broth I had prepared for her, and to take a cup of tea. After she had her strength back a bit, she told me that a witch down in South Carolina had cursed her after they'd had a disagreement over some small matter.

I write this now by candlelight, with Mother Blessing asleep again in her room, snoring softly. My spells have helped her, and she is of course powerful enough to help herself now that she's on her guard. But tomorrow I must leave for South Carolina, to find the witch and make her remove the curse.

Or else I shall have to kill her. Either way will work.

I remain,
Daniel Blessing, April 7, 1881

Kerry had just shut the journal and replaced the leather thong that held it closed when

Sonya and Dougie entered, arm in arm, laughing at some joke Kerry wasn't privy to. "Hey, Kerry," Dougie said by way of greeting. "That doesn't look like any textbook I've ever seen. What is it?"

"It's an old journal," Kerry replied, not wanting to reveal any more than that. Dougie annoyed her—she considered him a typical frat boy but without the frat, all about using his college years to drink and party and have a good time, knowing that at the end of it his degree and his father's connections would guarantee him a good job even if he never set foot in a classroom. She didn't quite know what Sonya saw in him, but then she didn't know Sonya well enough to speculate.

He disentangled himself from Sonya and reached for it. "Lemme see."

Kerry jerked it away from his grasping hands. "It's very old," she insisted, "and fragile."

Dougie screwed his blunt, good-old-boy features into a mask of hurt. "Jeez, I wasn't gonna damage it," he declared. "I just wanted to look at it."

"Kerry's pretty protective of her stuff," Sonya told him. Kerry noted her tone, as if she were talking about someone who wasn't in the room.

"Just the stuff that needs protecting," she countered. "This journal is almost a hundred years old, and the paper is brittle. I can't let anything happen to it."

"It's okay, Kerry—chill," Sonya chided. "No one's going to mess with it. Dougie's just having fun."

"More than you are, it looks like," Dougie added. "Looks like you need a boyfriend, Kerry. You shouldn't be sitting around here on a Saturday night with some moldy old book."

"You don't have to worry about me," Kerry answered, wishing he'd just go away. She sat on her bed and picked up BoBo, her old childhood rag-doll clown. "I'm fine."

"Tell you the truth, Kerry," Sonya said, dropping her voice to a conspiratorial level, "we were kind of hoping you had gone out for a while, if you know what I mean."

Sonya's meaning couldn't have been more clear. *But do I want to do her that favor?* Kerry asked herself. *Do I want to clear out of my own room so she and her horndog boyfriend can have their fun . . . and maybe paw through my stuff—*

even Daniel's journals—when they're done?

Resigned, she gathered up the things she'd need to spend an hour in the common area. For about the millionth time since the semester had started, she wished she had a private room.

By the time she had settled on one of the couches in the third-floor lounge, Kerry was fuming. Two girls she knew vaguely shared another couch and spoke in hushed tones about a project they were working on together, but blessedly the TV was off and the faint smell of microwave popcorn that hung in the air when she entered dissipated quickly. She made it clear that she was there to study, not socialize, and she buried herself in the American history text that she should have been reading instead of Daniel's journal. The words seemed dry and lifeless to her, though, especially compared to the journals, or even more, to Daniel's voice, telling her things about her nation's past that had never made it into the history books.

Kerry was trying, really and truly, to immerse herself in school, to put Daniel and Season and the rest of it behind her. And Kerry was someone who did what she put her mind to—they hadn't called her Bulldog over the summer for nothing. So why couldn't she just focus on the work? Why did images of Daniel pop up, unbidden, every time her mind wandered? Why did she keep seeing Season in every blond woman on campus?

The whole situation was just incredibly frustrating. She turned back to the history text and tried to read about the landing at Plymouth Rock, but the words just turned to fuzz before her eyes.

Daniel was there, in her dream, looking just as he had in life. His long-sleeved white shirt was clean and crisp, tucked into faded jeans, the sleeves rolled back a couple of times over muscular forearms. His hair was long and windblown, and he was laughing, head thrown back, mouth open, teeth even and white, gray eyes crinkled at the corners and dimples etched into his cheeks. He stood on a hill, at a slight distance from Kerry; she couldn't reach him or even hear his laughter, which should have been booming.

She moved closer to him, or tried to. But

for every step forward she took, the hilltop on which he stood seemed to move back. She tried calling out to him, shouting his name, but even her own voice vanished before it reached her ears.

Then a fog rolled in, as if from offshore—thick and wet, blotting out the view, blocking Daniel, then the entire hillside. Within seconds Kerry was alone, an island in a sea of white mist. Then even she was gone, the mist breaking her body into ever smaller chunks until it had disappeared completely.

Kerry Profitt's diary, October 21.

And again with the nightmares, now. All I need, right? Having gotten rid of them once—thanks, I am now convinced, to the appearance of Daniel in my life—they are back, and, it seems, with a vengeance. This one wasn't even all that scary in itself—I mean, the imagery wasn't—but the overall feel of it creeped me out big time. Especially the way that Daniel was there, and then he wasn't, and . . .

Oh, never mind. It's different from the dreams I used to have, which I forgot as soon as they ended. And a year from now I won't remember what the dream was, and this entry will make no sense.

Which distinguishes it from the rest of my life how, exactly?

Now Sonya is sleeping hard and I am wide awake, pretty much giving up on the idea of sleeping tonight. Fortunately the laptop screen gives off enough light so I can type without turning on a light and waking her highness. And since it's fresh in my mind, I can't stop thinking about the dream.

Its meaning? Obvious, I think. I miss Daniel. He was taken from me. Duh. Bonehead psych, no brainer.

The part where I disappear? A little tougher, that. Losing my identity? Maybe.

And maybe I should e-mail Brandy for a more comprehensive analysis. She's the doc, after all. I have her addy—we all have each other's, and have sent a few around since splitting up back in SD after the summer. But not as much as I thought we might, almost as if everyone wants to forget what happened, wants to leave Season and Daniel and the summer of our discontent well behind.

And really, who can blame 'em for that? It pretty much sucked. Find a great guy, and he dies. Find out witchcraft is real and scarier than you ever imagined, and the baddest witch around has it in for your new BF. Find out he's been chasing her for almost 300 years, so you help him catch her, only to watch her kill him.

Yeah, summer means fun.

Okay, here's the thing. School is just not happening for me. Sonya . . . ditto. Aunt Betty and Uncle Marsh check in from time to time, but I could be gone from here for a month before they knew it. So really, what's keeping me here? Lack of someplace better to go?

Only, see, I have an idea about that, too.

I've been reading Daniel's journals. That's just about the only thing that's held my interest, in fact. And Daniel is lost to me.

But that doesn't mean that part of my life has to be lost. Mother Blessing is out there, in the Great Dismal Swamp. Season Howe is out there too, still at large, and now owing for yet another crime.

One that I take just a little bit personally.

So here's my theory. I find Mother Blessing, convince her to teach me witchcraft, and then I hunt down Season Howe and give her what she deserves.

Nothing to it, right?

But did I mention people call me Bulldog?

More later.

K.

3

". . . McKinley's policies, particularly his unwavering support of the gold standard, helped build confidence among business-people and limited the effects of the depression," Professor Crain declared. "Which, incidentally, cemented Republican domination until the 1930s, at which time they lost it, largely due to the much greater Depression, which had been the ultimate result. Short term, the economy seemed to be doing well. But the truth was, that period was called the Gilded Age for a reason. The rich got richer and the poor became ever more destitute, and the gulf between them had never been greater. Long term, that helped lead to a financial collapse that was the most catastrophic in our nation's history."

Rebecca tried to take careful notes when Professor Crain spoke. She had already learned that he mingled historical fact with personal opinion in his lectures, and while he welcomed analysis that differed from his, one had better be prepared to back up one's differences. In any case, she found herself agreeing with him more often that not. Word was, on almost any other college campus he'd have a reputation as a bit of an ideologue, but this was UC Santa Cruz, where nonconformity was the norm and strong opinions were highly valued.

Anyway, his lectures were always stimulating, and the difficulty of his essay tests, while legendary, helped keep her interested. Lately, she'd been having a harder and harder time even getting out of bed in the morning. Reynolds, their cat, had taken to sleeping on the bed with her in the mornings, and as the year progressed and the weather cooled, the cozy comfort of her quilt with a purring cat pressed against her became more and more difficult to leave. Knowing that to miss even one of Professor Crain's lectures would lead to certain disaster come midterms helped spur her up and out of the house. Three afternoons a week, after class, she worked at a local coffee shop called the Human Bean, and that was the other motivating element—if she couldn't make it to school, she likely wouldn't make work either, and she'd be fired long before she flunked out.

After class she stepped from the lecture hall, blinking in the bright sunshine. Hector Gonzales, a classmate she'd become friendly with, followed her outside. "Party tonight," he said as he sidled up beside her. "You got anything going on?"

She didn't. "I don't know if I'm up for a party," she said vaguely.

"It'll be fun. Two kegs, limited guest list—it's at a private house, some friends of mine. Not a frat kind of thing."

She knew that her hesitation stemmed from the same root as her disinterest in leaving the safety of her own bed. One never knew what might happen, around which corner doom might lurk. She'd never been brave, but she also hadn't thought of herself as a fearful person. She was well on her way to becoming one, though. She didn't want to turn into one of those people who were afraid to leave their own homes, but she felt that she was heading down that road. If she never left the safety of her room, she would be okay. It was other people, other places that were dangerous. She didn't want to become antisocial, but if that was the only way to stay safe . . .

She shook her head violently, and when she looked back at Hector he was staring at her with evident concern. "I'm fine, sorry," she assured him. "Just a little fried today."

"I was worried for a second," he said. "You aren't getting that cold that's going around, are you?"

"I don't think so," she said.

"So, what about later then?"

"Give me the address," she replied. "I'll try to make it if I can."

As it turned out, by nightfall she had talked herself into it. She hadn't been to many parties in the early part of this year, and they were, after all, an important part of the college experience. She found the address Hector had given her—a small, Spanish-style bungalow a few blocks from campus—and knew immediately it was the right place. Students spilled out the door into the yard, loud music chasing them the whole way. Strangers greeted her like old friends as she passed them and worked her way through the crowded doorway, looking for Hector. The air inside was thick with beer, hormones, and dance music.

When she found Hector, he was already beyond buzzed, and into the sloppy and obnoxious category. He sat on a couch with an empty bottle in his fist, staring right past her like he didn't even know her. Rebecca felt a twinge of regret—not that she thought she and Hector might turn into anything other than friends, but part of the reason she had come tonight was that she enjoyed talking to him before and after class and wanted to get better acquainted. Clearly, that wasn't happening.

Disappointed, she almost turned and walked out of the house without even having a drink. But the clot of people between her and the door had become almost impenetrable, and the music hammered her skull, so she spun on her heel and headed the other way, looking for a back way out. She was sorry she had come now, just wanted to get home where she belonged.

She pushed her way through a door that she thought led to the kitchen, but there was a girl coming out of it at the same time—a girl a year or two older than she was, Rebecca thought, tall and thin, with a curly mop of dark hair and bright, friendly eyes. "Hey," the girl said, regarding Rebecca carefully. "You're just what we need."

"We?" Rebecca echoed. "What we?"

The girl put a hand on Rebecca's shoulder and leaned close to her ear, as if sharing state secrets. "In the bedroom," she said, causing all sorts of images to flit into Rebecca's mind. "We're holding a séance."

"A séance?" Rebecca repeated. She could barely hear herself speak. "Don't you need, like, quiet and privacy for that?" The fact was, she didn't care what conditions might be required for a séance. She knew, better than these kids, certainly, what the supernatural was all about, and she wanted no part of it.

But the girl hadn't let go of her shoulder. "We'll have all the privacy we need," she assured Rebecca. "Everybody saw the freaky people go into the back bedroom; they won't dare come in. Anyway, there's a lock on the door. We already have four other people besides me, but we want an even number."

"Does that matter?" Rebecca found herself asking.

"I have no idea," the girl said. "It's Shiai's thing. She just sent me to get a sixth person— and a girl, 'cause it's boy-girl, boy-girl, you know."

Rebecca was torn. Mostly, she wanted to get out of here and go home. But she recognized that for what it was—*something,* she thought, *between fear and outright cowardice.* It was silly to be freaked out. These were just kids at a party, wanting to have a good time scaring themselves. The same impulse sent people to horror movies and Stephen King novels. Rebecca decided it wouldn't hurt to hang for a little while, see what these people were like. She could use some new friends, she knew, and maybe she'd find them here. The girl who had stopped her was certainly amiable.

"Okay," Rebecca said quickly, before she could change her mind again. "Lead on."

"I'm Amy," the girl announced, grabbing Rebecca's hand and tugging her down the hall.

"Rebecca."

"Good to meet you, Rebecca." Amy knocked twice on a door, then opened it. "We have success!" she called into a darkened room.

Cheers greeted her entry, and Rebecca started to feel glad that she'd decided to stick around. The room was lit by six candles, marking the six points of a star drawn on the hardwood floor with chalk. It looked more like a Star of David, Rebecca thought—an image she had grown up with—more than any kind of magical pentangle or anything she could remember having seen. But then, Daniel Blessing hadn't really seemed to go in for that kind of thing, and he was her only contact with actual magic. So maybe it was authentic.

A person sat behind each candle. As Amy had described, they were seated boy-girl. Amy pointed and named at the same time, and Rebecca struggled to remember to whom she was being introduced. "Brad, Shiai, Donnie, Mark," she said. "And I'm Amy, like I said. And this is Rebecca."

"Hi, guys," Rebecca said, feeling shy now that she was center stage. At least the room was too dark for anyone to see her blush.

"Welcome, Rebecca," Shiai greeted her. Even though she was sitting down, Rebecca could see that she was short and squat, with chin-length blond hair streaked with green. Her sweater was black and snug, her jeans frayed at the hems. "Come on in. Have you ever been part of a séance?"

"Not really," Rebecca answered. No séances, and the occult activity she had been part of she wouldn't talk about here.

"Then you'll fit right in," Mark tossed out. "Neither have we!"

"But I read a book about it," Shiai added. "So I know basically what we're supposed to do."

Rebecca sat on the floor at the one empty star point, crossing her legs like the others had. She remembered having seen Brad on campus; he was tall, probably six and a half feet, with hair past his shoulders, and so was easy to spot and hard to forget. The others she wasn't sure she'd ever seen. Donnie was handsome, dark-haired and olive-skinned, and Mark was a little on the goofy side, with a short brush of red hair, freckles, and a crooked smile that was friendly and funny at the same time.

The company was comfortable for her, but she still had mixed feelings about the idea of a séance. Though she couldn't tell them why, she knew that messing around with the supernatural was not the safe, casual game they seemed to think. Her only consolation was that she didn't really expect them to be able to accomplish their goal—if indeed they had a goal beyond sitting in candlelight together and telling what would amount to ghost stories.

There were a few more moments of laughing and joking, but then Shiai took the lead, putting a finger to her lips. "We need to be quiet and concentrate," she instructed. "We should all join hands."

Rebecca reached out to Mark on her right and Donnie on her left. Their hands were warm, and she noticed that Mark's trembled a little. Nervous about the séance, or about holding hands with a strange girl, she couldn't tell. *It's not like I've been holding hands with a lot of boys lately,* she thought. *Or doing anything else with them, for that matter.* But she kind of liked the sensation.

Shiai moved a seventh candle to the center of the star. "Focus on the flame," she said in a hushed voice. "Try to clear your minds of any stray thoughts."

She stopped speaking then. Music from the front room rattled the door, but Rebecca, in the spirit of the moment, tried to block it out, to concentrate her entire being on the flickering candle before her. After many minutes, the breathing of everyone around her had settled into a steady rhythm. She felt her own body's breath, her heartbeat, the heat of the hands on hers, and then even those things slipped away. She might as well have been floating on a cloud in a night-dark sky, staring into the glow of a faraway star. Sound lost distinction, filling the space around her like soft cotton but without meaning. She became cognizant at some point that Shiai was speaking again.

". . . part the veils between this world and the next, and give us a sign of your presence," she was saying. "Slip the ties that bind you to that world and appear before us . . ."

Rebecca stopped paying attention to the words and let them join the music as just a sound that filled the dark room. Gravity had lost its hold, space and time folded in on themselves, and still Shiai droned on . . .

And then the candle's flame leapt from its quarter-inch height to become more than a foot tall, its bright light blasting her darkness-adjusted eyes like a camera's flash. Amy shrieked and Mark let out a loud curse. Rebecca tightened her grip on him and Donnie, her heart suddenly thundering. *This isn't supposed to happen,* she thought, *or it's a trick of some kind, a fake candle.*

But when Shiai continued, her voice was different, tremulous, and Rebecca knew that it was no fake she was part of. "Now tell us who you are," she commanded. "We know that you are here with us—identify yourself."

The candle had only blossomed for a second, and then its flame had returned to normal. Rebecca stared at it again, its light seemingly diminished even more in contrast to the sudden brightness. As Shiai continued, her voice caught, and Rebecca glanced away from the candle at her.

And she saw—where Shiai should have been—a blond woman, older than Shiai, leaner, taller, with a distinct sense of poise and elegance.

Season Howe.

Rebecca screamed.

She felt hands on her—Mark and Donnie and Amy, crowding around, trying to comfort her. She dared another look, and Shiai sat cross-legged across from her, anxious and frightened. "What is it?" she asked. "What's wrong, Rebecca?"

"Yeah, you scared the holy crap outta me," Mark added.

Rebecca swallowed, trying to regain some composure. It was only Shiai, after all.

But for that moment, it had seemed so real.

"Nothing . . . I'm sorry," Rebecca said haltingly. "I should . . . I should go."

"But we're not fin . . ." Brad began. He let the sentence die. The séance, as far as Rebecca was concerned, was finished. The others could stay here as long as they wanted. Rebecca rose unsteadily to her feet, supporting herself on Mark.

"I'm really sorry," she said again. The others tried to soothe her, to reassure her that her outburst had not been a problem.

But it was a problem for her. She hurried from the party as fast as she could, out into the cool night air for the walk home.

It was not really Season, she thought, trying to convince herself. It had only been her imagination running wild, that and the retinal burn from the candle's flare, making her see Shiai in a different way.

Because if it had been Season, that would mean that the witch was somehow looking for her, tracking them on the astral plane or something like that.

And that would just be too scary for words.

After dozing for a few hours, Kerry got to work.

She skipped her morning class, staying in bed until after Sonya left. Outside, a leaden sky glowered angrily, so Kerry was just as happy to remain in the warm comfort of her own space. She tugged on a Northwestern hoodie and cotton drawstring pants, tied her long black hair back with an elastic, and began.

Her first task was to pull all four of Daniel's journals from the bookshelf and scan them for any references to the Great Dismal Swamp, or to Mother Blessing's cabin. There turned out to be very few of either, but whenever she found one with useful details, she made notes. She had always thought it an interesting coincidence that Daniel, like her, kept a journal, and concluded that it wasn't just coincidence, it was one of the factors that drew them together, one of the points of similarity that made them appreciate each other. Daniel's journals—*just like a man,* she thought—were long on incident and short on emotion, while her own diaries were almost all about her feelings and reactions instead of recounting what exactly happened in her life.

Gradually, though, piece by piece, she drew together a mental picture of the swamp and the route one would take to find Mother Blessing's cabin deep inside it. Of course, whether that mental picture would prove to be at all helpful was yet to be seen. Interestingly, according to his vague descriptions, the swamp didn't change much over the years, but Mother Blessing seemed to keep her cabin updated, enlarging it and modernizing it from time to time. It had started as a one-room trapper's shack, but in the most recent entries Kerry could find, from the mid-1970s, it was a four-room cabin that sounded almost luxurious.

Noon had come and gone by the time she finished her paging through, and she hadn't even had breakfast. Putting the journals away, she made a trip to the floor's vending machines and bought a prepackaged sandwich, some chips, and an orange soda. She said hello to the few people she passed in the hall, but avoided conversation. Her body was in Evanston, Illinois, but her mind was far away, and she wanted desperately to stay in that place.

Back in the safety of her room, Kerry went online and searched the net for information about Great Dismal. It turned out to be a national wildlife refuge, which she hadn't known, straddling the border between Virginia and North Carolina. Beyond some descriptions of its history and a few long, scientifically precise accounts of its wide array of flora and fauna, though, there wasn't much to be found that would help her. It was interesting that George Washington had organized a company that drained and logged portions of the swamp—that backed up Daniel's claim that George had personally cut down some of the trees—but it wasn't information she could use. She couldn't find any really detailed navigational charts, for instance, and nothing so helpful as a map to Mother Blessing's cabin. Not that she'd expected any such thing, of course, and a quick Google search showed no online references whatsoever to Mother Blessing. That was almost surprising, until she realized that Mother Blessing would probably have the power to maintain her privacy to whatever degree she wanted. Season Howe didn't turn up on Internet searches, and neither had Daniel, for that matter.

Again, though, she made notes. At one point she pushed herself away from her computer screen to rest her eyes, and realized that two more hours had passed. *If I put this kind of effort into my schoolwork, the year would be off to a much more promising start,* she thought. But then there was nothing about her schoolwork that struck her with the same kind of urgency.

Around four, the door opened and Sonya returned, wearing a fluffy yellow turtleneck and dark pants. She dumped some notebooks on her desk, looked at Kerry, and blinked a couple of times behind her big glasses. "Have you even left the room?"

"Once," Kerry replied.

"Obviously didn't bother to put on any makeup when you did," Sonya pointed out. "Are you sick?"

"I'm fine," Kerry said. "Just involved in something."

"What is it? You mean a project for one of your classes?"

"Not exactly." Kerry suddenly felt defensive. Not only would Sonya not understand—she would steadfastly refuse to understand—but Kerry didn't want to share this information anyway. If she was going to leave the campus, go to Virginia and find Mother Blessing, she didn't want anyone to know where she'd gone, or why. Possibly she'd tell her summer friends, Rebecca, Scott and Brandy, and Josh, all of whom would be more likely to get it than Sonya. But no one else—certainly no one who might tell Uncle Marsh and Aunt Betty when they came around looking. "It's more personal," she added.

Sonya shrugged. She had, Kerry thought, become good at that—just about everything Kerry did or said merited a shrug as far as Sonya was concerned. That was okay. She'd started off the year hoping they'd become friends, but it hadn't taken long to realize that that wasn't going to happen. Now she wanted simply to get along well enough to not have her plans actively interfered with.

"Yeah, whatever," Sonya said at length, crossing to her closet. "I just came to get a coat—Dougie and I are going to the game tonight. You want to come?"

It was Friday, a fact that had completely escaped Kerry's notice. That meant one of two possibilities: for the next couple of days, Sonya would either be away with Dougie a lot, which would be great, or she'd be cooped up in the room with Kerry, studying, which would stink.

There was, unfortunately, no way to know which it would be until Sonya volunteered the information. Kerry didn't want to call attention to her curiosity by asking directly. But she tried one vague query, just in case.

"No, thanks. I'm going to stay in and keep working, probably through the weekend. You got any big plans?"

"I'm going to play it by ear," Sonya answered. No help at all. With another shrug and a wave, Sonya donned her jacket and left again. Kerry turned back to the computer.

If Sonya was going to be in the way, that made getting out of here in a hurry that much more important.

Sonya and Dougie went out for an afternoon movie on Saturday, which gave Kerry the opportunity she needed. She had already identified what she'd need to take, so she crammed it all into a duffel: some changes of clothes, especially heavy sweaters and jeans, essentials like underwear and makeup, her laptop, Daniel's journals. Anything else she needed, she could buy. Her bank had Saturday hours, so she'd stopped there earlier in the day and withdrawn what she thought she'd need. Money wasn't a particular problem—if she wasn't going to be in college, then the insurance settlement that she had set aside for that purpose was up for grabs. And she believed that Mother Blessing's would be an education in itself.

Assuming, of course, she doesn't just throw you out, she thought. *And you can find her in the first place.*

Friday's gloomy skies had turned into a driving rain that snatched brown leaves from trees and glued them to the sidewalks and gutters, blown by an icy wind off lake Michigan. Kerry made a last pass at the room, making sure she was leaving only clothing and schoolbooks she could stand to lose, but nothing of a deeply personal nature. Then she called a cab. Under a yellow umbrella with green frogs emblazoned on it, she waited, half a block from Elder Hall's front door, until it came, its headlights slicing through the downpour. She hopped in as soon as it stopped, tossing her duffel onto the seat next to her, folding her umbrella, and resting it on its point in the empty footwell.

"O'Hare Airport," she told the driver. He was a thin man wearing a bow tie and a cardigan sweater, and when he smiled at her in his rearview mirror his teeth were full of gold.

"What airline, miss?" he asked politely.

She told him and he pulled away from the curb, his movements smooth and precise. "Have you there in a jiffy," he said. "Do you mind the radio?"

"Not at all." This seemed like an auspicious beginning to her trip—a cabbie who was considerate and also knew his way around town.

He turned the power on and heavy metal music blared from speakers in both the front and back seats.

He smiled again, flashing gold. "Too loud?"

"Maybe a little." Kerry dug at her ears with her fingers, trying to see if her eardrums had in fact ruptured.

"Sorry." He turned the music down until it was a dull roar. She'd been expecting a violin concerto, maybe even opera. But it was nice to know that people could still surprise her. She settled back into the seat, guitars clashing and drums banging, and enjoyed the short ride to the airport.

Once at O'Hare, Kerry paid the driver and carried her duffel inside. She made sure people noticed her, buying a copy of *Sports Illustrated* along with her gum, because a young woman picking that magazine would be more memorable than one who chose, say, *People* or *Vogue,* at one of the WH Smith shops. She got dinner at a snack counter, and she greeted maintenance and security workers with big smiles and cheery hellos. After spending a couple of hours there she went back outside to the ground transportation area and caught a CTA bus to downtown Chicago's Greyhound station.

On the bus, surrounded by working people heading to or from jobs, and now and then by students, Kerry felt a sudden rush of sorrow for what she was giving up. Any life resembling these people's, she had decided, was destined never to be hers. But she had spent years looking forward to college, to the things she'd learn there, the friends she'd make, the professors and books that would swell her intellect and experience. Instead, she was leaving all that behind for an uncertain future, and the loss of her once-imagined life tugged at her heart, like a slender shadow of the pain she still felt at the loss of Daniel Blessing.

At the Greyhound station, she was considerably less friendly, keeping her gaze downcast and her face blank. She posted a letter she'd written to Aunt Betty earlier in the day—a brief note, really, saying essentially, "Don't look for me, I'll be fine but out of touch for a while"—and caught a 3:15 bus to Madison, Wisconsin.

She had a seat by herself on the bus, but the two men sitting behind her, nattering on about seemingly every tiny thought that flitted across their minds, made her wish she'd brought a Walkman or iPod with her. Instead she turned to Daniel's journals and lost herself in his exploits for the four-hour bus journey. Panic attacks threatened to set in every time she thought about what she was doing, but Daniel's voice, as she heard it through his words, managed to calm her every time.

Madison was freezing. The bus station there was on a narrow strip of land between two lakes, and the evening air, dark already at seven thirty, felt arctic to her. She pulled the sweatshirt hood over her head and walked up South Bedford until she spotted a cheap motel, the Flamingo Inn—the kind of place where, she believed, no one would pay much attention to anyone else's business. The desk clerk sat behind a thick, scratched Plexiglas window, and Kerry passed cash through a slot to him. He coughed, grinned at her with yellowed teeth and rheumy eyes, and gave her a room key. After a quick look at the room—bed, dresser, TV, minimalist bathroom— she went back into the cold, searching for a drugstore to find what she needed. Again she paid with cash, and she carried her bag back to her underwhelming temporary abode. The desk clerk eyed her as she returned, leering at her as if she were some kind of runaway. In a sense, she guessed she was, but she didn't think of herself that way. As she climbed the dank, musty staircase to her equally unsavory room, she decided that the difference was that she wasn't focused on running *away* from anything. She was running *toward* something—toward a definite goal, a new future, a destination that she would recognize once she found it.

Inside the room again, she locked and bolted the door, took a long, hot shower, and then toweled off and found *Saturday Night Live* on the battered hotel TV. She wasn't really in the mood for comedy, but she wanted to drown out any noise that might issue from the Flamingo Inn's other guests or staff and get ready for bed. The day had been long and wearying, the emotional impact of leaving her old life behind was hitting her hard in these last few minutes, and she found herself suddenly near exhaustion, tears welling in her eyes for no reason.

And tomorrow, she knew, would be longer still.

4

Morning came all too soon, and with it harsh light spilling through curtains barely worthy of the name. Kerry groaned and forced herself out of bed, rubbing her eyes and biting back yawns. She had too much to do to allow herself to sleep in, even though the idea of opening her eyes to her wretched hotel room filled her with dread.

The night before she had shampooed her hair carefully—long, dark, lustrous hair she had grown out and tended for years. She almost had to choke back tears as she regarded her reflection in the mirror, knowing what had to happen next. From the drugstore bag she removed a pair of new scissors. *I can't believe I'm doing this,* she thought as she took six inches of her tresses into her hand. *But what has to be done . . .*

Before she cut, though, she drew her hand down three more inches. *No use getting carried away,* she decided. A *little* change was better than none at all. Anyway, there would be more to it than the cut. Once she'd snipped away the extra inches—and the split ends that had resulted from a couple of months of virtually ignoring any maintenance beyond simple shampooing in the shower—she took the blue temporary dye she'd purchased at the drug-store and worked it into her raven locks. She knew she couldn't do much about the color without bleaching first, which she wasn't will-ing to do. But she figured even this little bit would create blue highlights, which people would remember—and which people who knew Kerry Profitt would never associate with her. This was the theory she had developed of disappearing: be as completely unlike yourself as possible, and they'll never find you.

Of course, she didn't expect that a huge effort would be thrown into tracking her down in the first place. Aunt Betty and Uncle Marsh would make some kind of attempt, but when it came to putting money into hiring a private detective or anything like that, Uncle

Marsh would draw the line. She was nearly eighteen, and she'd written a letter saying she was going away intentionally and was fine— that would be enough for him. Really, her disappearance would make his life easier. No more trying to keep track of and care for a teenager he'd never asked for in the first place. No more having his wife's loyalties divided when they fought, which they had done with some regularity during the months she'd lived in their house. Uncle Marsh was a drinker, and when he drank he got obnoxious—loud and demanding and unreasonable. Aunt Betty— Kerry couldn't figure out if she admired this, or despised it—had learned to put up with it, to ignore him or cajole him or otherwise accept his behavior. Kerry never could, never even cared to try, and that attitude had caused plenty of tension around the place.

So okay, she thought, *maybe I am running away a little bit. Running from a life I didn't choose, one that was handed to me without any input from me. But it's what I'm heading toward that keeps me going.*

When her blued hair was dried, she put on a nondescript red sweater and jeans. Much as she loved her trademark red checkered tennies, she chose to leave those in her duffel in favor of plain leather hiking boots—better in Madison's weather, and not as memorable. She packed up the rest of her belongings and checked out of the hotel; the desk clerk was a woman this time, not the same guy as last night, which was what she'd counted on. She dropped the key into the tray under the Plexiglas window, and since she'd already paid cash there was no further transaction necessary. Then she took her duffel and waited at a bus stop until a city bus came along. After paying the fare, she sat on the bus for almost an hour, riding through one neighborhood after another until she spotted what she was looking for.

Happy Jack's Wheel World was one of those used car lots that was not associated with a new car dealership but was simply a wide parking lot crammed with various models of vehicles, from a faded pink Jeep to a plum-colored Toyota minivan that looked as if it had never been on the road. Prices were painted on cardboard signs and leaned up against the windshields of the cars. Kerry had never owned a car and didn't really know what used ones should cost, but these prices seemed reasonable to her. After she looked for about fifteen seconds, a man who could only be Happy Jack—his huge bulk resplendent in a sport coat the color of spilled mustard and plaid pants that could have blinded a pro golfer—came out of a small office, smiling as if to prove his identity.

He shook her hand with all the energy of a spastic squirrel. "Looking for some wheels, miss?" he asked, his voice higher than she'd have expected for someone so large. "I'm sure I can put you into something that's just right for you."

Kerry didn't want a long conversation with this guy. She wanted to get in a car and get out of Dodge, or at least Madison. Her inclination was toward something small and economical, not a gas guzzler—although the Jeep would have been okay too, except for the pink part. Too showy. The last thing she wanted was to call attention to herself.

Finally, she pointed at the minivan— absolutely the last thing she could picture Kerry Profitt driving. "I'll take that one," she declared.

Happy Jack chuckled wetly. "You want me

to wrap it up, or are you going to eat it here?"

Fifteen minutes later she drove it off the lot. Even paying cash, she'd had to do paperwork, and since she didn't have a fake ID, her name and former address were down on paper. She decided it didn't matter, though. She was still a long way from her destination, and from this point she would become untraceable, just a girl with bluish hair inscribing an arc across a corner of America.

Kerry Profitt's diary, October 23.

On the theory that big cities are more anonymous than small towns, I picked St. Louis to stop in tonight. I've been here before, of course—from Cairo, it's the nearest "big city," so it's where I'd go with Mom and Dad for special shopping trips, cultural events, museums, and of course the zoo. That was a long time ago, though—a lifetime. In THIS lifetime, on this journey, I picked one of the dozens of roadside motels outside the city, more or less at random—they all look pretty much the same, and while free HBO and in-room coffee are nice, I'm not inclined to use a pool, spa, or weight room, so one is basically as good as the next.

Outside my window trucks grind through their gears as they climb the ramp back onto the interstate. My route from Madison, in case posterity cares, was Interstate 90 to Highway 20 to Interstate 39 to 55, with a lunch stop in Bloomington and bathroom breaks whenever the urge struck. I don't have a schedule and no one's waiting for me, so I've decided to move as fast as I can without killing myself too much. I'll drive, I'll stop, I'll drive some more. I think I did as much driving today as in the rest of my life combined, but it was all highway and I got pretty comfortable with it. Tomorrow it's Interstate 64 east, which will take me all the way to Norfolk.

Then things get tricky. Daniel had said that the former site of Slocumb can still be found on some maps, but not on most standard road maps. Daniel's journals are a little vague on how exactly to get to his mother's hideaway—and anyway, even when he uses specific directions, it's usually not much more helpful than "turn right at the big tree." Which, by now, might be surrounded by bigger trees, or chopped down, or whatever. I guess the important thing is finding the Great Dismal Swamp, which is easy, since it's a national wildlife refuge and all, and it's on every map. Then somehow, once I'm there, finding my way to Mother Blessing. Which I'm sure won't be easy. But I'm equally sure that I'll do it. It's meant to be.

Yawn, stretch. Sitting behind a wheel for hours on end is hard—I don't know how those truckers outside do it all day and sometimes all night. I feel like I need to walk a couple of miles just to un-kink, but I'm too tired to try. After this I'm going to plug into the phone line and send an e-mail to the La Jolla gang, my fellow veterans of the Season hunt, and then take a hot bath.

Then bed. At least this room is cleaner and more comfortable than the one at the Flamingo Inn. Thank the goddess for anonymously institutional chain motels, I guess.

And hey, free HBO. Maybe I can watch while I sleep.

More later.

K., the vanished one.

Brandy went into the bedroom and shook Scott's shoulder. He moaned and turned over, looking up at her, his pale, narrow face puffy with sleep, eyes blinking blindly. "Put on your glasses," she instructed. "E-mail from Kerry. You've got to see."

"You can't read it to me?"

"You've got to get up anyway," she reminded him. Mornings had never been his favorite time. "You have a ten o'clock lecture. It's almost nine."

He stifled a yawn, grabbed his glasses, pushed back the covers, and swung his legs off the bed. His chest was bare, with striped cotton pajama pants covering his legs. Scott was not a particularly impressive physical specimen, but Brandy liked him and the sight warmed her heart a little. Once he was upright she took his hand and led him into the living room, where the computer monitor glowed patiently. Rubbing his eyes, he sat down on the chair in front of the desk, and she read it again over his shoulder.

"Guys," it began, "I'm dropping off the radar for a while. I'll be fine. Please PLEASE don't worry about me. And don't try to find me (not that you would). I'll be in touch when I can. Where I'm going, what I'm doing, is very important—I think to all of us. I'll tell you about it (broken record here) when I can. Summing up: DON'T WORRY. WHEN I CAN. And I love you guys. K."

Scott read the e-mail slowly, or maybe twice, before turning back to Brandy. "What do you think she's up to?"

"Like I'd know? You have the same information I do."

He rose from the chair, folding his arms defensively over his chest. "I wasn't looking for certainty, just speculation, Brandy. You don't have any guesses?"

Brandy shrugged. "It's Kerry. Who knows how that girl thinks? If I understood her, I wouldn't have been so shocked to find out she and Daniel were, you know, a thing." It continued to annoy Brandy that she hadn't guessed that, since she liked to think of herself as a good judge of character and an astute amateur—for now—psychologist. She had known there was a strong connection between them, but she hadn't realized that it had blossomed into anything physical or romantic. By the time Kerry let on, Daniel was already dead.

She suspected that it hadn't been just romance driving Kerry's feelings. Kerry had lost her father, years before, and then nursed her mother through a long and difficult illness. When they'd found Daniel Blessing in their front yard, he had been injured, near death, and Kerry had once again been drawn to nursemaid duty. Brandy thought that some of what she'd felt for Daniel had been projection, layering her feelings about her parents, who were beyond her help, onto him.

"It's something to do with Season," Scott suggested, worry tightening his voice. Rebecca had called on Saturday afternoon, telling them about the Season sighting she had had—which she had later thoroughly discounted—at a party the night before. She had convinced herself that the whole thing was a figment of her imagination, but she'd been a little freaked by it anyway. She said she'd tried to call Kerry but there had been no answer at her dorm room. Now, apparently, they knew why. "She wouldn't do something like this unless it was. She's got a lead on Season."

"You're probably right," Brandy agreed. "I don't see her getting so worked up over anything else."

Scott's lips were pressed together in a tight line, and he looked at Brandy as if she should have some kind of answer. "We've got to help her."

"Did you read the girl's e-mail?" Brandy countered impatiently. "I'm talking about the part where she specifically tells us not to."

"Yeah, but—"

"But nothing, Scott. She says not to worry about her, and not to try to find her. So your response is, let's worry and then go looking?"

"Of course she'd say those things, Brandy," Scott argued. "Kerry isn't the kind of girl to say, 'Please worry about me.'"

"But you don't think she's the kind of girl who'd ask for help if she needed it?"

"I guess she would. Maybe."

"That's right, Scott," Brandy assured him. "Kerry's not stupid. She knows she can't take Season on by herself—hell, she knows all of us together couldn't take Season. She's not going to do anything rash."

"I suppose."

The good thing about Scott was that Brandy knew all the buttons, all the levers. He could be brought around to her point of view on just about any matter Brandy cared to make the effort on. There was, she thought, a certain amount of satisfaction and comfort in that—in knowing that when it counted, she could have her way.

Manipulative? Maybe. But with a purpose.

And as far as I'm concerned, getting what I want is a good purpose.

5

In addition to Roanoke Island, there was another small town on the eastern seaboard that suffered a mysterious fate, albeit more than a hundred years later.

Slocumb, Virginia, less than a dozen miles from the North Carolina state line, was founded in or around 1641 by John Slocumb, one of the earliest settlers to exhibit any interest in the forbidding region that came to be known as the Great Dismal Swamp. Slocumb, a trapper and explorer, led a group of settlers forty-some strong from the Jamestown colony to this new settlement on the edge of the Swamp, where it was believed oysters; beaver, mink, and deer hides; and alligator skins could provide a steady income for those willing to work hard and brave the Swamp's uncharted depths.

In 1665 the tiny village of Slocumb experienced a bit of a population explosion when William Drummond, then governor of North Carolina, discovered the lake which still bears his name, and commercial activity, mostly trapping, really began to take off.

But from a high point of seventy-some residents, in the spring of 1704, Slocumb's population suddenly—apparently in the space of a few days—dropped to zero. No one seems to know quite what happened, and there are no records to explain the mystery. What is known is that there was a great fire, which not only burned down the township but also ignited the eastern edge of the Swamp. No surviving Slocumbites, if there were any, were ever reported after the fire. Volunteers from the nearby towns fruitlessly battled the blaze off and on for a month's time before giving up on it completely, and they claimed that the fire had overrun the town, burning every structure to the ground.

Mysterious, unpleasant rumors began to spread about what may have happened to Slocumb's populace, including stories of massacre by Indians or runaway slaves, the infernal workings of witches and devils, and the awful idea that everyone in town had been caught by surprise when the fire broke out at night and thus burned to death in their homes.

Whatever the cause, no attempt was ever made to resettle the town's site.

—Edginton's History of the Coastlands, 1937

Kerry spent her third night on the road in Portsmouth, Virginia, where there was a library in which she was able to find a reproduction of a map of Virginia from three centuries before. Of course, the roads that existed now weren't shown on it. But she got a sense of where Slocumb had been, and by comparing that to current maps and skimming through some histories of the Great Dismal Swamp area, she pinpointed where she thought its site must be.

Not sure what to expect there, she bought an inflatable boat, plenty of insect repellent and sunscreen in a handy combination form, a couple of flashlights and batteries, and some portable food and water. It crossed her mind that a gun might not be a bad idea, given that there were wild animals in there. But she hated guns, and she decided she wouldn't sacrifice her principles for a measure of comfort that might be illusory. Anyway, if the place really was a wildlife refuge, shooting at the critters was no doubt frowned upon. Better to just watch her step and not take stupid chances.

Except, the whole thing's a big fat stupid chance.

Fully outfitted, she drove the minivan down Highway 17, past the tiny town of Deep Creek. The main occupations here seemed to be fishing and selling cold beer. Kerry figured that in hotter weather, the cold beer would be a popular item. Even now, it was quite a bit warmer than it had been in Chicago or Madison; there seemed to be some sort of Indian summer thing going on. The people she saw from her van were mostly men wearing T-shirts or short-sleeved shirts, many open over chests burned brick red from years of exposure to the hot sun.

Not far to the east of here was the Intracoastal Waterway, a series of inland channels upon which one could navigate all the way from Key West to Boston, if one had a boat and the inclination. Kerry had the boat—well, *a* boat, though she doubted that her little rubber dinghy would survive such an ambitious journey. And, she had to admit, she also had a little curiosity about the idea of traversing the country north to south on water without ever sailing open ocean. But that adventure would have to wait its turn. She had another one in mind for now, and who knew how consuming it would turn out to be? Maybe if she and her boat survived it, they'd try the Intracoastal next.

After Season Howe had been dealt with.

This region was notable, too, because it was the part of the country she'd been studying in her history class before she made the decision to leave Northwestern. Roanoke Island, the colony that claimed the first child of Europeans born in North America—and from which the entire settlement's population had mysteriously disappeared without trace—was on North Carolina's Outer Banks, just a short distance across the state line. She'd always been fascinated by that story, and by the cryptic word *Croatan* that was found left behind in their wake. That had all happened before Daniel was born, she realized, but maybe not before his mother was. Yet another reason to find Mother Blessing.

Finally, she found the spot on the roadway that she was searching for, a turnoff unlabeled except by a mile marker a dozen or so feet before it. She took a narrow lane that led off the highway to the right. Tall reeds towered over the van on both sides of the road, creating the impression that she was driving into a tunnel of some kind. Ahead, all she could see past the tops of the reeds was a wall of trees that looked impenetrable from here. Already, just moments after leaving the main road, Kerry felt as if she'd left civilization far behind her and ventured into some primeval world.

The road wound to the right and then left again, but always leading basically west, away from the sea and toward the heart of the Great Dismal Swamp. Kerry didn't know the names of any of the trees or plants she saw, but their effect on her was overwhelming—everything was green and incredibly lush. *This must be the most fertile spot on Earth,* she thought, *or one of them, anyway.* She'd never been very successful at growing houseplants, but from the looks of things around here if she'd had some of the local climate, soil, and water, she'd be queen of the green thumbs.

She drove with her window rolled halfway down, the warm air brushing her left arm and cheek thick with the rich, fecund aromas of the Swamp. The edge of the road was pebbled, and beyond the stones, the reeds stood in murky, stagnant water. The whole experience was like nothing she'd ever seen—or smelled.

After another ten minutes or so, the road came to an abrupt end. For a moment Kerry's heart fell; she thought she'd figured the way incorrectly or made a wrong turn. But then she spotted an old, unpaved track, made impassable to cars by the trees that had fallen across it, but still clearly something that had been considered a road at one time. Now it was little more than a space between trees, choked with weeds and brush, leading into the darkness of what looked like impenetrable jungle.

This was a development she hadn't counted on. But then this whole trip had been made without a real plan, just flying by the seat of her pants. No reason this part of it should suddenly be easy or predictable. Bringing the van to a halt at the edge of the roadway, right tires on the graveled shoulder, she was sure it wouldn't be.

The heat surprised her. When she'd been driving through it, her movement had made it feel comfortable. But now that she stood in it, listening only to the ticking of the Toyota's engine and the cries of unseen birds, it settled around her in a great, damp blanket of humidity. Clouds of gnats swarmed around her like manifestations of the temperature. She flapped her hands at them, then remembered the combination sunscreen/insect repellent in the van and went to retrieve it. A few moments later, suitably slathered, she braved the elements again. Gnats still crowded her, but kept a slightly greater distance; the sun, filtered as it was through the overhanging trees, still hammered mercilessly upon her.

The stretch of old roadway through the trees was relatively short, and after less than fifteen minutes it stopped, opening onto a wide clearing at the other side of which, Kerry supposed, the Great Dismal started up in earnest. On the far side of the clearing, the woods looked dark, benighted in spite of the early hour and the pounding sun.

But it was the clearing itself that struck her the most. This, she surmised, was the lost town of Slocumb. Not a building stood, but the blackened remains of charred timbers still rested where they had fallen back in 1704. Outlines were visible where once houses had been, and among them the paths of the lanes that connected them. The whole thing looked like a carefully preserved archaeological site.

What was most remarkable about it, though—the part that made her body shiver, in spite of the heat—was the fact that there was not a blade of grass, not a single weed—much less the mass of trees and roots and reeds and ferns that covered the rest of the landscape—anywhere within the confines of the Slocumb site.

It was as if a manic gardener had picked the site clean. The pathways between buildings were sandy and rock-strewn, and there was evidence of broken, crumbled oyster shells everywhere. The burned, skeletal remains of the buildings were as free of vegetation as the lunar surface. Even the air smelled different, lacking the musky, dank aroma of the surrounding swampland. Instead, it had a kind of sour stench that made Kerry think of the meat that had spoiled in her mom's freezer when a power outage had kept the electricity off for three days. Kerry hesitated to enter the space, but after a moment's consideration decided that she had to. All of Daniel's directions into the swamp had been from the other side, where the town site bordered the Great Dismal.

She shook off the sense of unease, as well as she could, at any rate, and ventured into the clearing. The air felt thinner here, rarefied, and maybe five or ten degrees cooler than the humid air outside the space. *This,* Kerry suddenly knew, *is the work of Season Howe. She did more than destroy the town; she put some kind of curse on the land so it would never recover.* It was no wonder the history books tended to ignore Slocumb—how could anyone explain this lifeless anomaly in the midst of one of the country's greatest swamps using only the limited vocabulary of science and accepted belief?

When she reached the first dwelling, its boards long since petrified as fire-blackened cinders, Kerry realized something else about this place. There was no noise here, not even the bird cries that had been omnipresent since stopping the van; no frogs croaking or crickets chirping could be heard from this place. And the cloud of gnats that had followed her every step of the way, even after she'd slathered on the insect repellent, had stopped at the edge of the clearing, refusing to enter. Only Kerry was foolish enough to tread this ground, it seemed. The silence was unnerving; the complete absence of life nearly terrifying. The tiny hairs on her neck and arms stood on end, as if Kerry had been subject to a jolt of electricity. She tried to swallow her fear and walk on, but her steps, instead of being courageous and determined, were small, hesitant, and she tried to keep a clear path at her back in case sudden retreat was called for.

Perhaps an archaeologist foolish enough to brave the place might have found something of worth in the ruined buildings, but all Kerry could see were ashes and scorched logs. The ground was solid beneath her feet, less spongy than the trail she had taken here from the van, but even so the people who built this village hadn't used stone foundations. A few piles of rocks that might once have been chimneys lay here and there, but rocks big enough for building seemed impossible to find—probably if they existed at all they had long ago sunk beneath the waters of the swamp. So for the most part, the construction had been wood, which had all burned.

After what seemed like hours, but was probably not more than ten or fifteen minutes even at her cautious pace, Kerry reached the other side of the clearing. Here the forest rose up thick and menacing, with patches of thorny blackberries filling in the space between tree trunks. She saw no way to walk through that morass without a machete, which she didn't have, and even with one the going would be slow.

But between the clearing and the trees was a narrow ditch filled with water that looked like soup, a dark, reddish brown color. Leaves floated on it, and it rippled in spots where there may have been submerged objects. It was maybe a dozen feet across at its widest point, and only half that right where she stood. She couldn't get a sense of how deep it was, even when she tossed in a handful of pebbles from the clearing. They simply plopped against its tranquil surface and disappeared. After rimming the clearing, though, the ditch turned to the west and disappeared into the trees, which meant, Kerry believed, that this was the waterway that Daniel had taken to his mother's house in the swamp so many years before.

Which also meant, she knew, that it was the path she had to take.

She'd left her supplies in the van while scouting the lay of the land. Now she regretted that decision, for it meant crossing the clearing twice more. But there was no other way to reach the ditch, at least none that she could see—the forest was impenetrable on every other side of the town's site. Biting back terror, she steeled herself and turned back, back onto the most forbidding piece of real estate she had ever imagined, back through the silence and the utter absence of life.

6

There's this theory that the weight of any object is inversely proportionate to how useless it turns out to be—the less one needs it, the more it ends up weighing, and vice versa. So the flashlight I brought with me weighed about an ounce, or maybe a negative ounce, since the inside of the Great Dismal Swamp at night is so ridiculously dark, but the can of beans I brought, because beans on a camp-out just seemed right, weighed about forty pounds. Had I brought a can opener, it might have dropped to just five or ten pounds—even less if I liked beans to begin with.

Okay, the theory is one I just made up. I don't think that invalidates its scientific truth, though.

Here's the thing. I maybe should have bought the Jeep instead of the van, because maybe I could have driven a bit closer to the barren stretch of land that used to be Slocumb. But I didn't, which meant I had to leave the van where it was and carry all my gear, including the inflatable boat, which—the exception that proves the rule—weighed about a thousand pounds more than it had in the store. Eventually I had to put some of the stuff down and make multiple trips to the ditch at the edge of town (or rather, former town), which I had decided was going to be my pathway into the depths of the Dismal.

Eventually, though—and ask me if I mind saying that walking back and forth across that bizarre, haunted piece of land was freaking me out in a gigantamous way, because it was—I had everything where I needed it. The boat, wonder of wonders, inflated when I pulled on the goobie, just like it was supposed to. And it didn't even sink when I loaded all the junk in it, like the forty-pound beans. If I'd had a bottle of champagne I'd have christened it, except for the part about how shards of glass from a broken bottle would probably shred an inflatable boat, and the other part about how I don't drink, but at this point in my admittedly bizarre journey I might have considered taking it up.

So without christening I just launched. No

motor or anything, sadly—it was all driven by Kerry-power. Me and my little toy oar, which was really too small to be useful, but fit in the box with the boat. At first it didn't seem too bad, but after a while it started to get old. And then when the over-hanging brambles and branches and logs (and other names for spiky wooden things) started hanging down so low over the ditch that I pretty much had to lay down in the boat to keep from hav-ing my scalp ripped off, rowing became that much harder.

Plus, did I mention the dark? Scrolling back. Yep, mentioned. But hey, if ever there was some-thing that merited repetition, it's that. Seemed like it would have been kind of late evening, in the real world, but inside the Swamp where the sun just doesn't reach, it was full dark way before I was expecting it. When I realized the light was going I looked around for someplace relatively dry and flat to stop, not wanting to spend the night on the boat. And after a while I found it—found this, in fact, the lean-to under which I am sitting and running down my laptop battery.

And what else is interesting is the way insects are drawn to laptops, which, who knew? I wonder if Mac has a way to clean blood and guts off the screen, because they keep committing suicide by slamming themselves into it.

Before the juice runs out, then, a summary of my position. Somewhere in the middle of the Swamp, except I don't know precisely where. I didn't exactly watch for the landmarks I read about in Daniel's journals because I was too busy watching for someplace to spend the night, which means that even if they still exist, I might have missed some of them, which means that I might be hopelessly lost. And I don't exactly know where I'm supposed to be going anyway. In spite of the insect repellent, I am being eaten alive by bugs. The Swamp makes strange noises—rustlings and hissings and moanings in addition to the more recognizable croaking and chirping, and I think it's really things in the Swamp, not the Swamp itself, which is actually a lot worse.

And all this gab is just a way of not admitting that I am freakin' SCARED TO DEATH out here . . . which, you know, who likes to admit that? But then again, it's the truth, so why not?

The books say people used to get lost and die in the swamp on a fairly regular basis. If I don't find Mother Blessing, will I die out here? If I do find Mother Blessing, will she turn me away, which could still mean dying out here? Or will she take me in like I hope she does? What is she like, anyway? I could write about that for hours, but the battery will never last.

More later.

K.

Mother Blessing was a surprise.

Kerry had begun to think she'd never find Daniel Blessing's mother. The Great Dismal was just too big, too dense, too full of dangers. She saw a black bear her first morning out; fortunately, the bear saw her, too, and turned back the way he had come, vanishing down a trail that seemed too narrow for a human, much less a huge furry beast. She had barely reined in her galloping heart when the creek before her, wider now and flowing faster than when it had merely been a ditch, parted to reveal an alligator drifting to the surface a few feet ahead of her. Kerry had a quick mental picture of it tearing into her inflatable boat with its razor-sharp teeth and sinking her, then finishing her off at its leisure. *This was a bad idea,* she thought, *a stupendously bad idea in a lifetime chock full of bad ideas.*

"I taste bad!" she shouted at the beast. "Really bad! That's what everyone tells me, anyway. Kerry, you taste bad. And you smell funny too."

Apparently she was convincing enough, because the gator drifted past her without biting her boat. For a couple of hours after that, she started to get used to the swamp, even to enjoy it. Tall trees arced over her head, creating an effect like a green cathedral. The fragrant forest floor was festooned with wide-leafed ferns. Butterflies and birds flitted and flew; squirrels scampered up the sides of trees; great multihued spiders spun webs like fishnets between tree trunks. There was a quiet charm to the place that she appreciated in a way she would never have expected the night before, when she had been so afraid she had barely managed to sleep at all.

As the day wore on, her nearly sleepless night began to catch up with her, and the beauty of the swamp combined with the gentle motion of the boat to lull her into a kind of stupor. So when she first noticed the men watching her from the banks, she didn't think anything of it. After a couple of minutes, though, she realized that there was something wrong about it. Men shouldn't watch her here—she was a unique enough sight in a place like this that any other human would hail her, not simply observe from the cover of thick underbrush. She tried to focus on the spot where she thought she'd seen one of them, but he was gone. Maybe a leaf shuddered slightly with his passing, or maybe it was a wisp of a breeze that moved it.

But Kerry was on the alert now, wide awake, senses sharpened. If she saw anything else she'd be ready.

Or so she thought.

The creek forked, and Kerry chose to go to the right. But though she paddled that way, the current had another idea, and it pushed her toward the left. She thought she remembered something in the journals about the right fork, and she tried to fight the pull. She lost the struggle, though, and gave it up after a few minutes, concentrating instead on keeping the boat steady against the sudden surge. It was more important not to capsize than to worry about which fork she should take when, for all practical purposes, she had no idea where she was or where she should be.

Just when she had the little boat settled on the water, Kerry caught another glimpse of movement through the thick trees. For a moment she thought it was a deer, or maybe— her heart pounded in fear—another bear. *What are you supposed to do in the event of a bear attack?* She tried to remember. *Make noise? Play dead? Run like hell?* Making noise seemed like the easiest, especially since trying to run might involve drowning, or a close-up encounter with an alligator or a water moccasin. For a moment she thought maybe she'd be okay if she stayed in the boat and the bear was on land, but then she remembered pictures of bears standing in rushing rivers, fishing for lunch. *So much for that idea.*

She brought the little paddle up out of the water and laid it across the boat's bow, trying to sit very still to minimize any sound. Maybe it hadn't noticed her at all. Through the trees, another flash of motion—something big and dark—caught her eye. This time she heard a noise, too, a rustling of leaves.

So it's not just shifting shadows.

As quietly as she could, she slipped the paddle back into the water and rowed for the opposite bank. The banks on both sides were sheer, with trees right to the edge, roots erupting from the cutaways. She wasn't sure where she'd be able to climb out of the boat, but she wanted to at least have a chance if some creature came at her.

The foliage across the water shifted again, as if something with serious weight were coming through it in her direction. That was all it took to spur Kerry. With two more powerful sweeps of the oar she made the far bank. There was a rope tied to a ring at the boat's bow, and she quickly looped it around the root of a tree. Then, setting her feet widely for best balance, she stood, clutching at a narrow tree trunk for more support. Putting one foot up on the bank, she hoisted herself from the boat and slid between two trees just as the dark figure on the far shore loomed into view.

It was not a bear, but a man.

Everything she'd read about the Great Dismal rushed back into her consciousness: a haven for people dodging the law, runaway slaves before the Civil War and Emancipation, and for criminals in every age, as well as a prime spot for hunters and fishers. If the man across the way had innocent intent he'd have said something by now, surely, not approached her with stealth and silence.

The ground under her feet was soft and spongy, the trees close together, with ferns and trailing vines covering the lower reaches and tangles of thickets tearing at her legs. Placing her feet was difficult, but she didn't intend to just stand there and let someone sneak up on her. As fast as she could manage, she pushed her way through the underbrush and around the trees, putting distance between herself and the creek. Once she had a rhythm going, she was able to get up a reasonable speed.

She was going so quickly, in fact, that she didn't, at first, notice the man who stood in front of her. When she did, it was too late—he swung something heavy at her and she tried to dodge, but a tree trunk blocked her way. A flash of light accompanied the impact, and then everything went dark.

I have to be dreaming, Kerry thought. *This can't be real.*

She seemed to be in an actual bed, with crisp, clean sheets pulled up around her. A dull ache throbbed at her right temple, but it wasn't any worse than an average headache, and there was none of the nausea she might have expected given the fact that she had apparently been clubbed into unconsciousness. The odors around her—she hadn't yet opened her eyes— were clean, almost antiseptic, not the pungent aroma of the swamp. And there were two exceedingly strange sounds: one a kind of electrical hum, and one a labored, artificial-breathing noise, as if Darth Vader were standing beside the bed holding a small appliance.

Or a light saber.

Having gathered as much—seemingly contradictory—information as possible, Kerry opened her eyes.

The first thing she saw was a woman smiling at her from a motorized scooter-style wheelchair. She was an enormous woman in her fifties or sixties, big in every way, from her teased, bleached beehive of a hairdo to her vast bosom and belly, barely confined in a plaid smock the size of a pup tent, to the thighs straining royal blue polyester stretch pants. A clear plastic mask across her nose and mouth was attached by tubes to oxygen tanks mounted on the scooter's rear. The scooter had wide rubber tires and a shallow basket mounted on the handlebars.

"Welcome back, darlin'," the woman said, her Southern accent thick as the trees in the Great Dismal. "I've been wonderin' when you'd be joinin' me. I'm so sorry for the way my boys brought you here."

"Here?" Kerry asked weakly.

"My house, of course," the woman replied. "Y'all were lookin' for me, weren't you?"

Kerry tried to raise herself up on one elbow. "You . . . you're . . ."

The woman breathed loudly into her mask, and then favored Kerry with another broad, slightly grotesque smile. "Folks call me Mother Blessing."

7

"Scott," Brandy said, her tone arch. "What are you doing?"

He turned away from the computer screen. "Checking e-mail."

"Didn't you check it, like, an hour ago? And an hour before that? Since when have you become compulsive?"

Her arms were crossed over her chest and her lips were pressed together so tightly they practically disappeared. Her stance, the tilt of her head, and the tone of her voice put him instantly on edge. "Well, it's just . . . you know. I'm hoping we hear something from Kerry."

Brandy made a tch noise and shook her head ever so slightly. "She said she'd be in touch when she could, right? I'm sure she's fine."

"Yeah, but we don't know that. And if we don't check, how are we going to know if she's trying to get in touch?"

"I swear, sometimes it seems like you think about that girl more than you think about me," Brandy said, turning away from him.

Scott came out of the chair and went to her. "You know that's not true, Brandy," he said. He wrapped his arms around her, but there was nothing yielding about her flesh; she didn't lean into him. Her velour top was soft, but that was just surface. It was like trying to hug a velvet bag of saw blades.

The thing was, maybe she wasn't wrong. "You know I love you, babe."

"You keep telling me so," Brandy admitted. But what she left unsaid was whether his words were convincing to her.

"I do," he assured her. He was about to say more, but the computer chimed softly, indicating an incoming e-mail. He felt Brandy's muscles tense even more. He rubbed a shoulder that seemed to resist his touch, and then returned to his seat. "It's from Josh," he said, unable to keep the disappointment from his voice.

When Brandy spoke again, she sounded distinctly uninterested. "What does he have to say?"

Scott scanned the message. It was short; their friend hadn't heard from Kerry either. "I'll read it," he said. "'Hey guys. Just checking in. School is, you know, school. Grades are fine, so no worries there. The rest of life keeps plugging along. No significant other, although there are a couple of guys here who might be potentials. You have any news from Kerry since she went AWOL? I haven't heard a thing, and I'm a little on the nervous side. Love you, Josh.'

"See, I'm not the only one who's worried about her."

"I guess it's a man thing," Brandy said. "We women know we can take care of ourselves."

"Somehow I doubt that Josh's interest would be the same as mine," Scott pointed out. Realizing how that might be interpreted, though, he quickly tried to cover himself. "Not that I have any interest of that kind. Just, if I did, you know, Josh wouldn't. Kerry being a female and all."

"I understood you the first time," Brandy said. Her tone had gone from arch to glacial.

Scott wondered if it was possible to make more wrong moves in one relationship than he did in this one and have any hope of keeping it together. Before he could add anything, though, Brandy walked toward the bedroom. Her body was tight and confined and there was no invitation in the way she walked; instead he got a vibe from her that was somewhere between a shrug and a flipping of the middle finger.

Just as well, he thought. *Anything else I said would only have dug me in deeper.*

Mother Blessing's house, Kerry discovered, was as surprising as the woman herself. It looked like any average ranch house—hardwood floors, plaster walls painted eggshell white, oak cabinets and avocado-green appliances in the modern kitchen. But outside the windows, the gloom of the Swamp pressed up against it, and through the screens Kerry could hear the buzzing of insects and smell the Swamp's fetid aroma clashing with an indoor odor that reminded her of pine-scented cleaning solutions.

After giving Kerry a moment of privacy to pull on a voluminous pink cotton bathrobe,

Mother Blessing led her on a tour of the place, seemingly as proud of her house as a new mother might be of her child. With her motorized scooter making agile turns and pirouettes, the woman took Kerry from the guest room, in which Kerry had awakened, down the hall to the bathroom, pointing out her own master bedroom across the way, then further through the single-story house to a kitchen and dining room, and then past the entryway into a living room that opened onto a screened-in porch. Once Kerry had the lay of the land, Mother Blessing led her back into the kitchen, where she took a pitcher of iced tea from the refrigerator.

"Sweet's okay, isn't it?" the woman asked cheerfully. "I hope so, because it's hard to take the sweet out once it's in there, isn't it?"

Kerry thought she was still in shock from the attack, because this whole scene seemed more than a little surreal to her. "Yes, I . . . I suppose it is. Probably."

"Not that it can't be done," Mother Blessing went on, pouring tea into two plastic tumblers with bright, primary-colored polka dots on the sides. "Just about anything can be done, if one's got the determination and know-how, right?"

Kerry simply nodded. She wasn't quite sure how to broach the more urgent topics that were on her mind, such as Daniel's death at the hands of Season Howe or the attack, seemingly at the hands of Mother Blessing's accomplices, that had brought her to this place. *Not that this isn't where I was trying to get to anyway,* she thought, *but I'd rather have done it without the lump on the head.*

Mother Blessing rolled over to the dining table with the two glasses and a bag of Oreos in the basket mounted on her handlebars and parked herself on the one side that didn't have a steel-framed chair. "Have yourself a sit-down," she urged Kerry, sliding one of the drinks across the table for her. "I know y'all have had a rough few days, and my boys didn't help matters none, I'm sorry to say."

Kerry shrugged and took one of the chairs. She knew that both of Mother Blessing's sons were dead. "By your 'boys,' you mean . . ."

"Simulacra," Mother Blessing said matter-of-factly. "Y'all know what that is?"

"Daniel told me." Simulacra, he had explained once, were humanlike figures magically molded from whatever substance was near where they were needed—in this case, Kerry guessed, maybe from swamp muck, leaves, and branches. He had also said that they were kind of a specialty of Mother Blessing's. Now that his name had come up, she felt she had to tell Mother Blessing what had become of her son. "You know, about Daniel? That—"

"That he's moved on to the next plane?" Mother Blessing interrupted. The wide, toothy smile half-hidden behind her breathing mask didn't falter. "Yes, I knew right away. As soon as Season did it."

"So you know it was Season, too," Kerry commented. "I was there."

"You meant a lot to him," Mother Blessing said. "Soon as I saw y'all, I knew you were Kerry. That porcelain skin, the big green eyes, the dark hair—course, Daniel didn't say anythin' about it being blue, but I figure that could be new." Kerry was shocked; she hadn't known that he had been in touch with his mother at all during the time they were together. The impression she had had was that mother and son were not particularly close. But then it was clear there was still a lot about the Blessing family she didn't know. She swallowed, fighting back sudden tears.

"It is," she managed. "The blue. And the feeling is . . . mutual . . . about Daniel. You don't seem . . ."

Mother Blessing blinked at her, breathing heavily. Her oxygen tanks hissed softly. "I'm not as angry as you expected? People die—even *our* people. Even witches. It's a passage, that's all."

"Daniel said something like that too. But he still took it seriously. He never forgave Season for killing Abraham."

"Nor have I, child. Season has much to answer for. I mean to see that she does."

Kerry sipped her tea and watched Mother Blessing pull her oxygen mask aside so she could do the same. The older woman followed it with an Oreo. They might as well have been swapping recipes or hair-care tips, Kerry thought. "That's why I . . . why I came looking for you," she said. "I want revenge. On Season. For Daniel, and for our friend Mace, and for . . . well, everything. I want to see justice done." Kerry steeled herself, knowing her request was probably premature. "I didn't know myself why I wanted so badly to find you, but now I do. What I want is for you to help me . . . to teach me. To make me powerful enough to fight her."

Mother Blessing laughed suddenly, little bits of Oreo spraying the varnished wood tabletop. Her laughter shook her enormous frame and turned to coughing, then choking. Kerry was afraid the woman would die right here in front of her, but she didn't know what to do about it. Through her paroxysms, Mother Blessing snatched up her oxygen mask and held it over her nose and mouth until gradually she was able to control her breathing again. When she looked at Kerry again, mascara-streaked tears ran down both cheeks.

"Child," she said finally. "Y'all are a spirited one, aren't you?"

Now that she had declared her purpose, Kerry saw no reason to back down. "I'm sorry," she said, "but I am completely serious. Daniel said the craft could be learned, that one didn't have to be born a witch."

"Daniel was right," Mother Blessing agreed. "It's not easy, and it's not something that can be taken lightly. It can be done, of course. I'm not sure I'm the right teacher, though. My days of power are somewhat behind me, I'm afraid."

Kerry touched the side of her head where it was still tender. "Powerful enough to have me brought here unconscious by your simulacra," she pointed out. "And, I'd guess, powerful enough to have patched me up, since this doesn't hurt nearly as much as it seems like it ought to."

Mother Blessing made a dismissive motion with her hand. "Nothing," she declared. "A couple of herbs, an ointment. And I am sorry about the simulacra, child. They didn't rightly know who you were, did they? I knew you were tryin' to find me, of course—soon as you entered the Dismal, I knew that. But not the who or the why. If I'd have known it was you, my invitation would've been much more neighborly, wouldn't it?"

You tell me, Kerry thought. She didn't give voice to it, though. She was asking this woman, this utter stranger, for a huge favor. She didn't want to start on an accusatory note. Even if the woman had bashed her head in, however remotely. "I guess that's true," she said, accepting the semi-apology that Mother Blessing had offered.

"Of course I know a little about y'all," Mother Blessing went on. "Through Daniel. But even so, I don't know you myself. How do I know if I can trust y'all with the kind of power you're talkin' about, the kind that could make y'all a challenge to Season? How do I even know you haven't joined up with her?"

Kerry felt her face flush with anger. "I wouldn't!" she raged. "I couldn't team up with that . . . that . . ." She had been about to say "witch," but realized that in this company that wasn't necessarily a powerful epithet. So she just let the sentence trail off, knowing that her meaning was clear. "She killed the man I love."

Mother Blessing regarded her for a moment, silent. Then she nodded slowly. "So she did."

"You can't possibly believe I'd be . . . in . . . in *cahoots* with her or something."

"I'm just sayin' I don't know what to believe, child. I have years—centuries—of hate built up for Season. Y'all have, what, a couple of months? If I'm supposed to teach you what it takes to defeat her, I have to know you're goin' to stick it out. I have to know y'all are as committed as you say, don't I?"

"Well, I'm here," Kerry pointed out. "I left college, and everyone I know, to come here. I tracked you down—as well as I could, anyway, and if your 'boys' hadn't attacked me I'd still be out there in the swamp looking for you. I have—oh, crap!" She suddenly remembered her gear, which she'd left in the boat when she ran from the simulacra. "My boat—I have some of Daniel's journals in it, and my laptop!"

"That's all in the closet in the guest room," Mother Blessing assured her with a patting motion of her hand. "Don't you worry about that."

Relieved, Kerry blew out a sigh. "I've been reading his journals, studying them," she said. "Trying to learn as much as I can about Season, her habits, her weaknesses."

"I've got more of those journals here," Mother Blessing told her. "On that bookcase in the living room."

Kerry had known there must be more somewhere, since there were chronological gaps from book to book. "I'd love to read them."

Mother Blessing examined her again. Kerry felt like she was under a microscope, or an X-ray device—as if the woman were somehow looking beneath skin and muscle and bone to what lay deep inside, in the innermost reaches of her heart. "Maybe you will," Mother Blessing said. "Maybe you just will. You know, what you're askin', that's a lot of responsibility. I'm not as young as I once was, and I'm not sure I can keep up with a spirited little chickadee like y'all. Might could be a strain on my heart."

Kerry was heartened by this development. "Does that mean I can stay?" she asked, unable to keep the hope from her voice.

Mother Blessing didn't answer right away. Kerry understood that this was one of her conversational traits: taking a long time to answer, letting the other person feel off guard. Asking questions was another one, even though they weren't meant to be answered. This time, she did both.

"I guess y'all can stay on for a spell. We can get better acquainted before we make any big decisions, can't we?"

8

Josh Quinn's mother was downstairs in her home office, which was where she seemed to live these days. Except, her office, Josh knew, was also the location of her wet bar, and if what she did in there had anything to do with work, then she had given up her real estate license in favor of rehearsing for a role in a remake of *Leaving Las Vegas*. He'd tried to talk to her about it, but nothing doing. He'd even, for what it was worth, left brochures for substance-abuse clinics and a copy of AA's *Little Red Book* where she'd be sure to find them.

But she could ignore a hint just as easily as he could drop it. Maybe easier. All she had to do was pretend not to notice what she was dumping in the trash, whereas Josh had to actually go out and acquire the stuff he brought home for her. Most of it he found on campus without much trouble, but even picking it up and glancing at it meant acknowledging that perhaps he had an addiction problem of his own brewing, and—*like mother, like son*—that wasn't something he wanted to dwell on.

He shut down his computer and headed downstairs. He thought about calling Henry, a friend from school who he had believed might become more than a friend if the circumstances were right. Last time he'd called Henry for a date, though, the conversation had been awkward, and he had ended up not following through. Henry was attractive and articulate, and Josh liked him a lot. But on the phone the other night, there had been a sudden moment when Josh had realized that his friend's experience of the world was so limited that they were like residents of two different planets. They both shared an affinity for noir books and films, for instance. But Henry's entire understanding of violence came from pop culture, and when Josh objected to his hyperbolic comment that he'd like to kill one of his professors, he hadn't understood that Josh viewed killing and violent death through a more realistic lens than he once had. Josh had been unable to overcome that mental hurdle for a few minutes, and Henry had noticed his hesitation. Things had gone downhill from there, and Josh hung up a short while later, thoroughly embarrassed. Rather than put himself through that again, he decided to just go out by himself.

For a moment he considered putting on a light trenchcoat, but decided against it. He had on a long-sleeved black T, tight black artificial leather pants, and high boots with silvery buckles running up the insides, and he was pretty sure he'd be warm enough this evening. Stopping outside his mom's office door just long enough to call "I'm going out!"—and hearing no reply—he went out.

Downtown was a couple of miles from home, the Strip even farther. Tonight, though, he didn't want the slightly seedy, no-frills atmosphere of downtown. He wanted to immerse himself in spectacle, in themed entertainment as carefully thought out as Disneyland, albeit with a slightly different focus. The choices were many: Casinos were disguised as fantasy versions of New York, Rio, Paris, Venice, ancient Rome, medieval Europe, the high seas. He could mingle with acrobats and clowns at the circus or pharaohs in ancient Egypt. This time choosing none of the above, he hiked until he could flag a cab, then asked the driver to take him to the Mandalay Bay. He'd never quite figured out what its theme was—some sort of generic Balinese paradise that didn't quite have the courage to commit to its *Gilligan's Island* roots—and that ambiguity suited his mood tonight. Plus, he enjoyed the fact that sections of it had sunk sixteen inches into the ground after it was built, requiring hundreds of steel pipes bored into its foundation to stabilize it. Somehow that seemed to sum up the Vegas experience for him—just do it, and worry about the consequences later.

If Mother Blessing was a surprise, what Kerry saw when she left the house was even more of a shock.

The day had been exhausting, what with the not having slept much and the various excitements of traveling through the Swamp, including but not limited to being chased and clobbered by simulacra. So, despite her nap and the sweet tea's caffeine, after talking with Mother Blessing for a while, Kerry was ready to sleep again. Mother Blessing took her back to the guest room, showed her where her things had been stowed, and left her to get some rest.

Kerry tugged on a tank top and some pajama pants she'd brought, and climbed into bed, clutching BoBo, the clown doll that had made the journey with her. In spite of her exhaustion, though, the day's events echoed in her mind and sleep was hard to achieve. The double bed was comfortable and roomy, and she had two good pillows—a big improvement over the night before, when her bed was the ground in some hunter's ancient lean-to with the Swamp's wildlife investigating her—but still she tossed and turned for more than an hour before finally drifting off.

Once she finally succumbed, her sleep was deep and without dreams.

She woke early the following morning, when the Swamp was quiet and still and the day's first light was sending yellow streamers across a rosy sky. Curious, Kerry moved through the silent house, still clad only in her nightwear, and slipped out the front door. The Great Dismal seemed a different world from this angle, beyond Mother Blessing's slatted wooden walkway—magical and mysterious, though in a cheerful way, not threatening at all.

But when Kerry turned back toward the house she felt a sense of dislocation that almost made her lose her balance. She faced not a suburban-style ranch house, but a tiny swamp shack, something a trapper might have lived in during the few days it took to set a line of traps. The boards were old and warped, with spaces between some big enough for rats to pass through, the windows covered with what looked like nailed-down tar paper. The waters of the swamp seeped under the walkway right up to the walls, with trees pressing in against the cabin from three sides.

That's not what I came out of, Kerry thought anxiously. Worried that the whole house might have been a fevered dream, a result of the knock she'd taken to the head—or that it might have been real, but was gone now—she hurried back to the shack's front door, which was at least in the same place as the door through which she had exited. She threw it open quickly, and the scene inside the entryway was just as she remembered: nicely floored with hardwood, walls of eggshell white, a sideboard holding a series of potted herbs, and some framed still lifes hanging on the wall above it.

Confused, Kerry stood in the doorway. Inside was Mother Blessing's house as she remembered it, complete with the artificial pine scent of whatever she cleaned with. But when she stuck her head out of the door and looked at the outside, she saw the ramshackle cabin. The disjunction made her head hurt, so she gave up trying to figure it out. As she walked back to the guest room, Mother Blessing's bedroom door opened. Kerry waited for her to emerge, then described what had happened. She wondered if there was an explanation.

"What do y'all expect, child?" Mother Blessing asked her. "It's magic."

"But . . . which one is real?" Kerry pressed.

"That depends, doesn't it?"

"On what?"

"On if y'all are inside or out, silly," Mother Blessing said. She made it sound like it made sense, and Kerry decided to leave it at that. But she knew that she couldn't take anything about this place at face value.

Kerry Profitt's diary, October 26.

After showering in the hall bathroom and dressing in "my" room, I came back out to find that Mother Blessing was up to something in the kitchen that she didn't want me witnessing. Apparently the kitchen is not just where she dishes up the sweet tea, Oreos, and Scooter Pies that seem to be her primary food-stuffs; and by the way, how has she lived to this advanced age (though not necessarily in good health, given the ever-present oxygen mask, etc.) on such a diet? The kitchen is also where she practices her magic, or whips up her potions, or whatever she's doing in there.

Right now, I could go for a Scooter Pie. Or a steak. Yesterday I was too bushed to really care much about food, but today my hunger is catching up to me, and with the kitchen off-limits I only have the stuff I brought in my duffel to sustain me. I've had some trail mix, but the idea that there's a whole kitchen just out of reach is starting to consume me. I'm imagining a pantry stocked with everything I could ever want to chow down on, though in fact it's probably just loaded with more types of cookies, with maybe a few five-gallon jars of mayonnaise and some cases of Velveeta.

Maybe I'm being unfair, or stereotyping the poor woman needlessly. So far, though, I'm getting a really strange vibe from Mother Blessing. She doesn't trust me, that's clear—hence the no-admittance-to-the-kitchen-while-she's-working rule. But it seems like there's more than just that going on— she's trying to be a gracious hostess, I think, because she knows Daniel loved me and maybe because that's what Southern women do. I'd never have pegged her for a witch, though—look at me, Ms. Expert all of a sudden! For one thing, I would expect a witch to maintain herself in a healthier state. Daniel made it clear that he was something of an anomaly, that not all witches spend their whole lives either preparing for battle, battling, or recovering from battle, like he did. But it seems like she would have to be at least a little concerned about Season coming after her, even if she has no other enemies. And except for the simulacra in the Swamp, which seemed to have been dispatched specifically to find me, I haven't seen any defenses at all. Maybe the house's disguise helps with that, though I'm not sure how. If anything, it seems to create the impression of a defenseless place—something a good, stiff wind could knock over.

So the sense of Mother Blessing that I get, obnoxiously prejudiced as it is, is that she's a woman I'd expect to see wheeling her little cart through Piggly Wiggly, stocking up on Ding Dongs and Twinkies, rather than a witch of enormous power and influence.

But Daniel indicated that she was the latter—that when the Witches' Convocation comes around next year, she'll be a participant of considerable importance, though also one that Season might try to railroad in witchy court.

For Daniel's sake, I've got to see if there's anything I can do to help prevent that. But also, and more importantly, from my perspective, I've decided that what I really want is for Mother Blessing to prepare me to take Season on in battle. Daniel asked me not to seek revenge, and I'd love to honor that request. But the truth is, I'm not spiritually advanced enough for that. I guess I'm not as decent a person as he believed I was. Because as small and petty as revenge is supposed to be, it's what I want.

The idea of it is one of the only ways I've made it through these last months, since Daniel's death, with any sanity at all.

And of course the other aspect of it is that if Season is allowed to live, she'll keep doing the things she does. I don't have any illusions that now that she's killed Daniel, she'll suddenly reform. On the contrary—without him tracking her constantly, she might feel more free to wreak havoc wherever she goes.

She's got to be stopped. I don't know if Mother Blessing is the right person to help me stop her, but I don't have a whole lot of options at this point. So until she throws me out bodily, this is where I'll stay.

Haven't seen a phone line yet, so I can't call or e-mail my buds. I'll just have to hope they're doing okay and not worrying about me.

More later.

K.

Just when Kerry thought she'd either faint from hunger or be reduced to finishing off her camping supplies—which she had hoped to preserve in case she wound up back in the swamp—Mother Blessing called her into the kitchen. The smells that greeted her were heavenly, and she saw that Mother Blessing had prepared two plates with pork chops, dirty rice, greens, and mashed potatoes.

"I thought y'all might be hungry," Mother Blessing said with a welcoming smile. The oxygen mask hung from its strap around her neck. She delivered a couple of plastic tumblers of iced tea to the table. "Ready for supper?"

"More than ready," Kerry answered happily. "Starving, in fact."

"Well, sit yourself down, child," the older woman invited. "I didn't mean to leave y'all settin' out there by yourself for so long."

Kerry tried to set aside the anger she'd felt earlier. "I know you didn't plan to have a houseguest," she said. "I can't expect you to rearrange your whole life for me."

Mother Blessing parked her scooter at the table. "It's just a real busy time for me, honey. Just a few more days to All Hallows' Eve, you know."

Kerry didn't follow at first. "You get a lot of trick-or-treaters way back here in the Swamp?"

Mother Blessing laughed so hard that

Kerry feared another choking incident. "Goodness no, child," she said when she was able. "It's the most holy day in our calendar."

"Oh." Kerry felt embarrassed by her lapse. "Of course."

"If y'all are serious about learnin' our craft, you've got to know these things."

Kerry could barely contain her excitement. "Do you mean it? You'll teach me?"

Mother Blessing chuckled, but this time without near-asphyxiation. "Did I say that, child? I didn't hear myself say that. But I haven't ruled it out, either, have I? I'll give it some thought these next few days, and y'all think about whether it's what you really want. Once you start down that path it ain't so easy to turn around, is it? You don't want to get into something that you don't really want to see the finish of."

"I do, though," Kerry insisted. "My friends, during the summer? The ones who helped Daniel find Season? They called me Bulldog, because once I put my mind to something, I don't let it go. And there's never been anything I've been more dedicated to than this. I can guarantee that."

Mother Blessing nodded her huge head, that billow of platinum hair twitching around it as if it had a mind of its own. "I won't be surprised to learn the truth of that," she said. "Not at all, child. Not at all."

9

Mother Blessing has told me the story since I was old enough to pull myself to my feet with my tiny hands on her knees, but I realize now that I've never put it down on paper. Since she's not the type who ever would, I suppose, it falls upon me to do so, in case something should happen to me and it should never be told. Here it is, then, as she has told it—and of all the billions of people on Earth, she is the only one who would know.

Well, she and one other. But that person's version of the story, if she tells it at all, is surely not to be trusted. So the best I can do is to commit to history the facts as I know them.

At the dawn of the eighteenth century,

Slocumb was a village of industry and high moral standing. The village claimed seventy-six residents at that time, most taking their living from the Swamp, or farming the fertile land at its edges. John Slocumb had died but his family had stayed on, with two of his sons working his fields and a third hunting and trapping, living the life of a swamp hermit deep inside the Great Dismal. There were other families Mother Blessing knew well too: the Mortons, the Tanners, the Wallmers, and more.

Kerry sat back in Mother Blessing's leather recliner chair—which also, its owner had pointed out, tipped back almost flat, rocked, and had hidden rollers inside which would massage Kerry while she read, if she chose—and held the journal against her chest. Reading it, she heard Daniel's voice in her head, almost as if he were there with her again. Missing him was a physical sensation, an ache in her gut that faded from time to time, but never abandoned her completely. She wondered if everyone's first love was the same way, or if this was something unique to them. She had tried to broach the subject with Mother Blessing, but the woman had seemed uninterested in or uncomfortable discussing her son's relationship with a girl who was his junior by almost three centuries.

This wasn't the only topic Mother Blessing chose to avoid. While she had hinted that she'd be willing to teach Kerry witchcraft, she hadn't yet committed to a plan of action, or even allowed their brief conversations to drift back in that direction. Now she was back in her kitchen with the door closed.

Kerry had staked out her spot in the living room, anxious to read more of Daniel's journals and to learn whatever she could about his life and craft—especially here, in his boyhood home, where she almost thought she could sense his presence. There was a tall bookcase in the living room with a few random best-sellers from years past, as well as a stack of the heavy leather volumes that were obviously Daniel's journals. A TV stood in one corner with a lace doily on top and a potted plastic flower centered on that. Kerry didn't understand why anyone would have a fake plant in the middle of one of the most fertile spots in the country, but the list of things about Mother Blessing that she didn't understand was a long one. *The more I learn, the longer it gets,* she thought. *I didn't necessarily have an idea of what she'd be like before I got here, but whatever I thought, she isn't it.*

Besides the recliner there was a wrought iron couch that looked particularly uninviting, and, in the corner opposite the television, a straight-backed wooden chair that looked like something one might see in a Shaker household. The chair looked about as comfortable as sitting on a rock, but it appeared to Kerry to be very old, maybe dating back to the early days of Slocumb itself.

Which reminded her about the journal. She listened for Mother Blessing for a moment, but all she heard from the kitchen was a tuneless humming. She opened the book again.

> *The people of Slocumb didn't have a lot of time for fun and games. The Swamp provided for them, but not easily. They had to wrench their living from it, making use of its wood and water, its creatures, its abundant plant life.*
>
> *But while these were honest and hardworking citizens, God-fearing and sober, near the end of the century a darkness*

seemed to settle over the village. Crops failed, children died young, and even the Swamp seemed to turn against the townsfolk. A rogue bear came into town on several occasions, attacking, mauling, and killing. Alligators left the swamp and hid in the creek that ran along the edge of town, preying on swine, young cattle, and even people who strayed too near. Each incident seemed accidental, random, but they added up quickly; within the space of six months a full quarter of the town's residents were either dead or crippled in some way.

Once the extent of the devastation became known, rumors began to spread as to the cause. These were religious people, of course, but also superstitious and ignorant ones. So the explanations didn't revolve around bad luck or unhealthful environmental conditions, but swung to curses and witchcraft.

Living in Slocumb were two suspects: Mother Blessing herself, and Season Howe. Mother Blessing was known as a woman of extraordinary empathy and unusual talents. Season was less beloved, and little trusted by the townspeople. She kept to herself, living in *a small house where, it was said, inhuman creatures came to visit her in the dark of night, including the Devil himself on some occasions. Suspicions were voiced in whispers, but no accusations were made, no action taken.*

Then, one freakishly cold October morning, as a rare snow dusted the Swamp, a widow woman named Flinders woke to a silent household.

October, Kerry thought. *So this month is an anniversary, of sorts.* Mother Blessing hadn't said anything about that, and Daniel had never pinpointed a date when he told her the story, only mentioning the year. The thought of poor, as yet unborn Daniel and the horrible things that were about to happen to his hometown made her feel sad for him. But she kept reading, wanting to know more.

She had three children under the age of seven, born before her husband was killed in the Swamp by a bear who hadn't been as badly wounded as Mr. Flinders had thought. Most mornings the children were noisy, playing or squabbling in their room, but on this morning not a sound escaped their door, and when Mrs. Flinders went to look inside, a scene of unimaginable carnage greeted her horrified eyes.

Her three young ones were all dead in their beds, throats savagely torn as if by animal claws, blood soaking the bedding and pooling on the wooden floor. The window was wide open and a chill wind blew flurries of snow into the room. A scream caught in Mrs. Flinders's throat, and it wasn't until she crossed to the window and looked outside to see the tracks in the snow—animal tracks such as a wolf might make, she believed—that it finally broke free, shattering the early morning stillness.

Neighbors came running, and then the town's constable and two of its three clergymen. A hunting party was quickly gathered and the tracks followed through the snow that had fallen during the night. But at the Swamp's boundary the tracks suddenly disappeared, as if, the constable said, the beast had suddenly sprouted wings and taken flight.

The clergymen agreed that there could be only one explanation.

Witchcraft.

The names of Season Howe and Mother Blessing sprang to everyone's lips. The tracking party split into two, one branch heading for each of the suspected witches' homes. Mother Blessing was sound asleep beside her husband—my father, Winthrop Blessing—when a determined rapping on the front door roused them. Both grumbled as they opened the door to find Parson Coopersmith—a dour-faced man whose black clothes and ghastly pallor would have made him as suited for undertaker's work as for the pulpit—standing at the front of a pack of a half-dozen men armed with muskets, axes, and, in one case, a pitchfork.

Mother Blessing knew at a single glance that this could not be good news. The men's faces were grim, their eyes hard, and of course there were the weapons they bore. "What brings you here?" Mother Blessing asked without preamble. Winthrop Blessing, never a strong man, according to his wife's stories, stood mute beside her.

"There has been an incident," Parson Coopersmith declared. "The widow Flinders's

children have been murdered in their beds. Every indication is that witchcraft is behind it."

"Witchcraft?" Mother Blessing asked him. When she tells the story she says that she was acting like a natural performer, since she had never publicly admitted to witchcraft, though many in town knew her ways and came to her for help from time to time. "Then why come to me?"

"There are tales," Parson Coopersmith said diplomatically. "You and I have never had any troubles, Mother Blessing. But this . . . this has gone on too long, and we can no longer turn our backs on this activity."

"You believe my wife to be a witch?" Winthrop asked angrily, finally rousing himself. "And a murderer?"

"I believe her to be a possible witch," the parson said, "and therefore suspect in this matter."

Mother Blessing felt her confidence shake at this point. She well knew that it was not their responsibility to prove that she was a witch; rather, the accusation having been made, it was now her job to prove that she was not—an impossible task.

A couple of contradictory ideas came to her. She could run, though that would certainly mean giving up her home in Slocumb forever. She could fight—and win—but that would demonstrate her witchcraft beyond question, and even though these men would never talk, she wouldn't be able to keep their deaths a secret. Or she could go along with them and accept the task of proving her own innocence, which could not be done, since anything she said or did would now be suspect. There were, she knew, no good options. Time and circumstance had gone against her, and all the good she had ever done for the townsfolk couldn't save her now.

"Leave this house at once, Parson," Winthrop demanded, perhaps recognizing himself the impossible choice that confronted his wife.

But she ignored my father's outburst. "Allow me to dress properly," Mother Blessing insisted. "I won't meet my fate in my nightclothes, and you men should be ashamed for facing me in them."

There were murmurs of dissent from the

group, but Parson Coopersmith quickly and loudly overruled the others. "As you would, Mother Blessing. Make haste, though."

Mother Blessing closed the door on them. She could hear them arguing, some afraid that she would grow wings and fly out a window so they wouldn't be able to stop her. If she could do that, of course, she could have done so at the door just as easily. But they were frightened and superstitious, and she supposed that she was lucky no one with a musket had fired upon her as soon as she showed herself. She dressed as rapidly as she could, doing her best to ignore their fearful comments, while reassuring her anxious husband that she would be fine.

Of course, she knew that if witchcraft had indeed figured into the murders, like as not Season Howe was behind it. But one witch didn't talk about another, even in such a dire circumstance.

As it turned out, she didn't need to bring up Season's name. Another group of men had gone to Season's home, and her response had not been as calm and reasoned as Mother Blessing's had been. Instead, she had answered their accusation with the proof they sought, a powerful demonstration of witchcraft that killed them all where they stood.

Her assault was witnessed, however, and even before Parson Coopersmith and his group returned to the town center with Mother Blessing, an alarm had been sounded. From every corner of Slocumb men ran toward Season's home, only to find themselves beaten back by her magical blasts. Parson Coopersmith and his men heard the commotion and charged forward, dragging Mother Blessing along with them. Winthrop armed himself with a musket and joined the group.

Mother Blessing tells me that as they neared Season's the very quality of the air changed. There was so much magic in the air the color of the sky was affected, purpling over Slocumb even though it was early morning, and a smell like burning skunks filled the town. Her guess was that Season had lost control of herself—that in her rage or terror she had unleashed so much magic that it was feeding her own extreme emotions, which then spurred her on to greater efforts in an ever escalating cycle of destruction. Those who had first approached her were all dead now, as were any others who had been nearby.

And still it continued. Parson Coopersmith raised a cross toward Season and advanced on her, shouting out a prayer with every step. But Season uttered words in the ancient tongue and gestured toward him, and a moment later his head was ripped from his body and sent flying, rolling to a stop near Mother Blessing's shoes. The body stood a moment longer, and then dropped the cross to the dirt and collapsed.

Panic spread through Slocumb at that point, and those who had given thought to attacking Season changed their minds. Instead of going after the witch, they ran for cover. Season didn't care, though. Mother Blessing saw her standing in front of her home, her pretty face twisted in unreasoning fury, unleashing wave after wave of incredibly powerful magics. Dust swirled away from Season, choking the streets, and a ferocious hurricane-force wind picked up, bending trees and tearing shingles from houses.

Mother Blessing tried then to stop her. Except for Winthrop Blessing, who proved to have some backbone after all, the men surrounding her had all run away, leaving her exposed in the road. She had left the house empty-handed, though, not anticipating a challenge like this. She tried a few spells, but they were blown back from Season by the furious power of the other witch's magic.

Mother Blessing realized at that moment that even she was powerless to rein in Season's wrath. Season Howe had lost all sanity, all the rationality that normally kept her in check. There was no stopping her now, not unless she could somehow calm herself down. And that didn't seem to be happening. Finally, even Winthrop was caught in her attack: he picked up a fallen musket and fired a ball at her, but Season simply reversed its course, driving it through his skull with enough force to shatter it, blowing bits of brain almost all the way into the Swamp.

Lashed by wind, stung by flying dust, pummeled by chunks of wood and debris, and agonizing over the death of her hus-

band, Mother Blessing had no choice but to retreat. She escaped into the depths of the Swamp, from which she could still hear the screams and cries of dying villagers, could smell the smoke as one building after another caught fire in an inferno that burned in the Swamp for more than a month.

By the time Season's preternatural tantrum quieted, two days and nights had passed. Mother Blessing dared to venture from her safe haven only to find the town leveled, the swamp ablaze, and every last soul in Slocumb dead. Except her, and the two unborn in her belly: my brother Abraham and myself. Season, who had caused the destruction, whose rage had destroyed a town, was gone.

And Mother Blessing dedicated her life, and those of her sons, to hunting her down. That task continues.

I remain,
Daniel Blessing, March 23, 1797

10

Rebecca Levine walked away from campus toward her shared Victorian, her loose, flowing batik skirt fluttering against her legs in the gentle breeze, her soft peasant top open at the neck. She caught glimpses from time to time of the Pacific shimmering in the distance. She had always loved the ocean, loved the natural beauty that surrounded Santa Cruz. But the ocean now reminded her of La Jolla, and that reminded her of Season Howe and Daniel Blessing. Rebecca had never seen anyone killed before—didn't even like violent movies and TV shows—and the sight had been utterly horrifying. She wanted to surround herself with grace and beauty, to forget the vision that would not be forgotten.

She found herself thinking about it at odd

moments. When she was sitting in class, listening to even the most stirring lecturer, she would suddenly realize that her mind had drifted, that she was back on that street in San Diego, watching Season cut Daniel Blessing down with her mystical attacks. Or else she would remember the séance at which Shiai had turned, momentarily, into Season— though she had persuaded herself that she had been carried away by the moment, that it had just been an awful hallucination. Sweat would pour down Rebecca's sides, her fingernails digging into her palms, her heart pounding. She knew her grades were suffering because of the stress, knew that she needed to pay better attention in class, but she couldn't force her mind to comply.

When things had been tough during her childhood, Rebecca's mother had had an odd habit of reminding her that her great-grandparents had survived the concentration camp at Buchenwald. "If you think your life is really so hard, think about theirs for a while," she would say. "Then maybe you'll understand that your problems aren't as big as you think."

It had worked, most of the time, when she

was a kid. But then she'd been part of a big family—mother, father, and three brothers—and there was always noise and activity going on that she could use to bring herself out of her occasional funks. Now she didn't have that, her problems seemed far worse than they had ever been, and even thinking of the great-grandparents she had never met didn't quite do the trick.

When she reached the house, she was covered with a thin sheen of perspiration; Indian summer had brought a heat wave to northern California and the walk home had been hot and dry. The house was dark, it was cool inside, and she was almost to the refrigerator for an Odwalla when the phone rang. There was an extension mounted on the wall in the kitchen, so Rebecca reached it almost immediately.

"Hello?"

"Rebecca?" The voice sounded familiar, but strange.

"Kerry, is that you?"

"Yeah," Kerry responded. "It's me."

"Where are you?" Rebecca asked anxiously. She hadn't heard from Kerry since that cryptic e-mail—hadn't even had a chance to tell her about the séance. Now that they were actually speaking, though, it seemed unimportant. "You sound so weird."

"It's a little hard to explain," Kerry said. "And I don't know how much time I have. I'm calling via the built-in microphone on my laptop, since there's no phone here. Or phone line, for that matter."

Rebecca didn't understand. "So then what are you on? Cable? Satellite?"

"I don't really know myself," Kerry said. "But if I had to guess, I'd say magic."

Rebecca felt herself blanch. "Kerry, you're not . . ."

"I'm fine, Beck. Really. Don't worry about me. You know I can take care of myself."

"But why are you messing around with magic?" Rebecca asked.

"Someone's got to stop Season," Kerry said flatly.

"But . . . you?"

"I don't know if I can," Kerry admitted. "But I know that if I don't prepare myself and try to do it, I'll never succeed."

"I guess that's true," Rebecca said. She felt like there had to be something she could say to her friend to change her course, to make her realize what she was doing. Kerry was brave and capable, and she'd seen for herself what Season could do—had felt it more than the rest of them, Rebecca was sure, because she and Daniel had been in love. Even so, she thought, maybe Kerry underestimated what she might be getting herself into.

"Listen, Beck, I'm being way careful. I'm learning witchcraft—Daniel's mother is starting to teach me. I'm not going to do anything rash. I just wanted to let you know how you could get hold of me—assuming this connection keeps working. Like I said, I'm not really sure how it's working now, since there aren't any lines connecting the computer to anything."

She told Rebecca she couldn't be telephoned. Or if she could, she wasn't sure how, but that she could check e-mail again at her existing e-mail address, and probably could call if necessary. When Kerry disconnected, Rebecca was confused all over again. How could she get email without being connected to the Internet? But they had spoken, somehow, so clearly the physical laws that she had once believed in didn't apply here.

Having promised that she'd let the others know how they could reach Kerry, Rebecca booted up her own computer and sat down to write one of the oddest e-mails she could remember.

Mother Blessing had emerged from the kitchen while Kerry sat in the living room trying to fathom what it must have been like to be the last living person in Slocumb, with the homes smoldering pits of ash and coal, the bodies of her husband and friends and neighbors strewn everywhere, acrid smoke painting the air, and a layer of ash overlaying everything. "Are y'all ready?" Mother Blessing asked before Kerry even knew she was in the room.

Kerry started, closing the journal she still had open on her lap. *Is it time for dinner?* she wondered. She knew time had passed while she'd been reading, but she had no idea how much. "Ready for what?"

"Your first lesson," Mother Blessing said.

"Really? Do you mean it?" Kerry asked excitedly. This was why she'd come, what she'd been waiting for. But instead of teaching her a spell or mixing a potion, Mother Blessing sent her into the Great Dismal Swamp to look for a particular type of plant.

Slogging across the wet, uneven ground, Kerry felt more like a lackey than a student. Mother Blessing had shown her a picture of the plant she was looking for—a white, five-petaled flower with broad green leaves—given her a bag, and instructed her to bring back a sack full of its roots.

"The craft is as much about knowin' the natural world around us as anything else," she informed Kerry. "Our swamp here is a bounty of blessings, but y'all have to know what to ask of it, and how, and it'll help you when it can. Ain't a better place on Earth for a witch to find what she needs, or if there is I'd like to know about it. And there ain't a better way to get to know it than on your hands and knees."

The task took Kerry the rest of the afternoon, and by the time she returned to the house—still ramshackle ruin from the outside, suburban spotless on the inside—she was soaked, cold, scratched, bug-eaten, and miserable. But she had her bag of roots. And that's when Mother Blessing surprised her with the laptop setup, which she promised would be able to communicate with the Internet, even though she wouldn't explain just how. Kerry tried it out for a few minutes, retrieving e-mails sent to her account over the past many days, then using her built-in microphone to try calling her friends. The first one she was able to reach was Rebecca. She knew Rebecca would contact the others and talk to them, and she felt more comfortable spreading the word that way than sending out e-mails she wasn't sure would get through, or that might be magically intercepted somehow. Kerry didn't know if Season Howe kept track of Mother Blessing, but just in case, she didn't want to do anything that might bring Season's wrath down upon them.

At least, not until she was ready.

After a hot shower and a filling meal, Kerry followed Mother Blessing into the kitchen. Mother Blessing set two cutting boards out on the table with two sharp knives and the bag of roots. When Kerry sat down across from her, Mother Blessing took up one of the knives and one of the roots and, with skillful, precise movements, skinned the outer surface of the root, revealing a moist, white interior, which she tossed into a ceramic bowl. "This is the part we need," she said. "The outside's nothin', might as well be bark. The power's in here, where the root takes in nutrients from the soil, takes in water, and transmits it all up into the body of the plant. A plant's just like a person, has to eat and drink in order to live and grow, doesn't it?"

Kerry almost laughed, thinking of the fried foods and soft drinks and sweetened tea that Mother Blessing seemed to live on, wondering how long a plant would survive on a diet like hers. She was the last person Kerry would expect to give lessons on nutrition—even plant nutrition. But Kerry knew better than to give voice to such a comment. Mother Blessing seemed to be beginning her lessons, and Kerry didn't want to interrupt her, especially with something that might be considered insulting.

"What's the connection?" she asked, picking up her own knife and a section of root. "Between witchcraft and things like plant roots. I just don't quite get it."

"Our power doesn't come from us, child," Mother Blessing explained. "Or from the Devil, as some would have you believe. It comes from the Earth, through the Earth. It comes from the plants and animals and the rocks and the sky and the water. Some call the source the Goddess, or Mother Nature, or other names. But it's all the same in the end— we don't possess the power, we just channel the power that's around us all the time. That's why I wanted y'all to start getting used to nature— really muckin' around in it, y'know, instead of just moving blindly through it like y'all have been doin' your whole life."

"I haven't been . . ." Kerry started to object. But then she gave it a moment's thought and realized that she probably had been. She had always been drawn to the beauty of nature, the rivers near her home in Cairo, the ocean, the trees and skies and mountains she had seen. But seeing beauty wasn't the same as knowing nature, as being on a first-name basis with it. Kerry thought that that was what Mother Blessing was getting at, and why she had spent the afternoon in the Swamp, digging through mud with her bare hands, uprooting plants. "I guess you're right," she said after reflecting.

"Y'all are gonna find out I often am," Mother Blessing said, with a chuckle.

Kerry held her piece of root toward the pot, its outer surface scraped away, its inside liberated. "Can I taste it?" she asked. "Is it poisonous or anything?"

Mother Blessing shrugged. "Find out."

Kerry raised an eyebrow. That seemed like the hard way to learn a lesson. *But hard lessons stick, right?* She brought the root to her lips, opened her mouth, touched it to her tongue. It was bitter, and a little on the hot side. Not especially pleasant, but she didn't think it would kill her. With the knife she cut off a tiny sliver; she put it on her tongue, feeling its heat, then swallowed it. "I hope that wasn't a bad idea."

"Well, we'll just see if you live or die, child," Mother Blessing said casually. "I expect it'll be live."

"Let's hope."

"Unless, of course, you harbor evil thoughts, right?"

Kerry raised both eyebrows at that. "What if I do?"

"Then it could be bad," Mother Blessing said. She was very matter-of-fact about the whole thing, still carving up her roots.

"But . . . doesn't everyone?"

Mother Blessing laughed out loud. "That's right, child," she declared. "Lesson number two. And three. Life, and magic, are about balance, including the balance of good and evil that exists in all of us."

"That's two?" Kerry queried. "So then what's number three?"

"Don't ever let 'em get you down. Even if they're your teachers. Or your enemies. Psychological warfare, Kerry. It's as important to us as spells and magics. If I'd have let y'all think you'd eaten poison it could've actually made y'all sick to your stomach."

"Like people who believe they're cursed, so they exhibit the symptoms of the curse?"

"That's right." Mother Blessing tossed another root into the bowl. "Sometimes they just believe it. Then again, sometimes they don't believe in curses, but they get the symptoms anyway. Because sometimes the curses are real, aren't they?"

"I . . . I suppose sometimes they are."

"Better believe it," Mother Blessing said, her tone suddenly serious. "Sometimes they're as real as can be."

11

Kerry Profitt's diary, October 31.

So it's Samhain, which Mother Blessing pronounces
SOW-waaain, stretching the final syllable out in her
Southern way. I've always just called it Halloween,
and thought it was all about trick-or-treating and
gorging on candy, but apparently there's a lot more
to it than that in the Blessing world. This is one of the
most important nights of the year in her calendar, up
there with the solstices.

She says I get to celebrate with her tonight, but
first I had to have another lesson in the Swamp. She
gave me a chart and my little skiff and sent me to Lake
Drummond, the biggest body of water within the
boundaries of Great Dismal Swamp. There was a jug in
the boat that I was supposed to fill with water from the
lake. The best tasting water on Earth, she said, because

of the cypress trees that constantly freshen it.

"Magic is all in how y'all use the energies that surround us, child," she said when she was giving me my instructions. "Energy is everywhere—how else would trees grow, and the grass, not to mention people? It's how rocks form, how wind blows, how water runs. The world is full of energy, and most people walk around in it without even knowing it's there, much less how to use it. That's where our kind are different." She stopped then, and laughed like she does, a high-pitched kind of titter that seems strange coming from someone her size and age. "Well, like I'm different, anyway, and it won't be too long for y'all now, will it?"

"I don't know," I told her. So far we had been talking only about theory—she hadn't yet SHOWN me anything, or told me how to do anything except chop up roots. In a way it was a complete reversal—Daniel had shown me plenty, but told me precious little. He hadn't, of course, shown me much by way of demonstration; it was mostly just him doing what he had to do to keep me safe. "Will it?"

"Let's us get through tonight, Kerry Profitt," she said—the first time she ever used my full name, I believe. "Then we can see what we see."

Which I took to mean that after Samhain is over,

she'll start teaching me the good stuff. So I went out into the Swamp—it had cooled considerably over the past few days, and was starting to feel like fall outside—and followed her directions. This time I was less scared than I had been before, and more attuned to the world of the Swamp. It's a green world, every shade imaginable and then some. From the thickets at foot level to the tops of the tall trees blocking out the sun, green is the predominant color. I know that if I study with Mother Blessing long enough I'll learn the names of all these trees, and more than that, I'll know their properties: what they can do, what they can provide. I saw, moving about in the trees, a stunning array of birds—black, gray, brown, white, blue, yet more green. Also squirrels, a flash of fur that might have been a fox, and several alligators floating through the still water like sentient logs.

Instead of traveling through the swamp worried or frightened, this time I passed through it in a state of wonder, breathing in the rich, fertile aromas, listening to the burble of the creeks, the calls and whistles and shrieks of the birds, the buzz and whisper of insects, really SEEING everything for the first time. Mother Blessing's directions were as clear as if the boat itself knew where we were going—which, hey, maybe so, considering who we're talking about—and Lake Drummond was amazing. I dipped my head down to it and drank some of the water straight from the lake, and she was right—I've never tasted anything so fresh and sweet. Rimmed by trees, like castle walls around a big, calm pool, the area was quiet as death, which is a creepy kind of simile—or at least that's what I would have thought before talking to Mother Blessing so much. She is a little strange about death. She misses her sons, but she says that death is just another part of life, just a passage, which Daniel also told me. She says death returns a person's energy to the world, so ultimately it's a good thing. Hard for me to see it that way, but maybe in time I will.

Going back to Mother Blessing's was almost, in a strange way, disappointing—like having to go back inside was punishment because it meant I couldn't stay outside. The sun was lowering, though, and I didn't want to be out in the swamp alone at night, and I especially didn't want to miss the Samhain celebration. She's in her room now, getting ready, and I've washed the swamp muck off me and am just waiting, and waiting . . .

More later,

K.

Las Vegas on Halloween night was a zoo. *Worse than a zoo,* Josh thought, *because in a zoo the animals are contained. In Vegas, they're everywhere.* The Strip was clogged with traffic, and Josh had to shoulder his way through the homeless people, tourists, and partyers filling the wide sidewalks that served no function except to connect the huge casinos. The lights were always glaringly bright here, the cars in the streets always loud, the people always determinedly cheerful, but with an edge of desperation, as if they knew they were expected to have a good time here and thought if they didn't that it was because of some personal failing on their part.

But on Halloween, it was all magnified a hundred times. Walking into the Mandalay Bay, where he had found a slot machine he particularly enjoyed because it seemed to like him, he saw people in costume—women mostly, though a few men as well—drinking and gaming and carrying on all around him. There were an inordinate number of cops around, but tonight they were all female, and their uniforms consisted mostly of hot pants and low-cut, figure-hugging tops, with high heels and maybe a nightstick or a pair of handcuffs hanging from their belts. But it wasn't all police officers: There were similarly sexed-up firefighters, nurses, and maids, and among the men pirates and pimps seemed to be the themes of the moment. For a change, laughter and loud voices clashed with the familiar electronic chiming, dinging, and clanging of the casino machines.

Recognizing that his usual Goth look—augmented tonight by a belted black trench coat that Humphrey Bogart would have worn proudly—could be construed by some as a costume, Josh hugged the casino wall until he reached the bank of slots where the machine he liked was located. It was called the Whirlwind, and whenever two like objects showed up on the pay line, whichever wheel didn't match went into action again, spinning around like mad to give the player one more chance at three matches across. One could play up to three coins at a time, with jackpots commensurately larger the more a player put into the machine. Josh hadn't had any huge payouts, but he'd left the other night with sixty dollars more in his wallet than he'd started with. Tonight he had two rolls of quarters in his pocket, no early classes the next day, and the intention of making his money last for a while.

His first five quarters were no go—he might as well have tossed them down a storm drain. On his next coin, he won two credits. He put in another quarter and played all three. Zero. Ditto the next four bucks. This was turning out to be not nearly as enjoyable nor as lucrative as the other night. Of course, there was still an advantage to not being at home, either listening to his mother get wasted or fighting with her about taking better care of herself. That was a pretty big plus.

By the time he had reached the last coin in his first roll, he was lighting one smoke after another with his Zippo, waving away the cocktail waitresses in their skimpy outfits, and trying to ignore an obnoxiously loud couple—she in skintight black leather, he in a Laughlin T-shirt, baggy shorts, and a Utah Jazz ball cap—who were either flirting or fighting but apparently hadn't decided which they wanted to go with. Barely twenty minutes had passed—at this rate, he'd be through all the money he'd brought with him in no time, and therefore reduced to either going home or finding someplace where he could hang out for free. And most of the free options didn't pass his annoyance threshold test.

He started to dig into the pocket of his black jeans for the second roll of quarters but stopped himself as soon as his finger touched it. Obviously, the machine was cold. The Whirlwind had worn itself out for now. It needed a breather, and so did he. He left the machine, giving it some time to get its mojo back.

Instead of going right to another game, he wandered into the big lounge in the center of the playing floor. The live band had taken a break, which was good since he couldn't stand their watered-down version of rock music. He didn't order a drink, but instead drifted at the edge of the drinkers, listening to snatches of conversation and looking at the wild Halloween outfits. Throughout most of the casino the circulation system whisked virtually all odor from the air, but here a cloud of smoke hung thick and heavy.

"Video discs," he heard one man say to his companion, a bitter edge in his voice.

"What about 'em?" the other man asked.

This man was in his sixties, gray hair long and curled at his shoulders, wearing a Western-style jacket and a bolo tie. The first man looked to Josh like a businessman on casual Friday—he wore a neat polo shirt, khaki pants, and deck shoes and had both a cell phone and pager clipped to his belt.

"I was all set," he said. "Perfectly positioned. Big, beautiful store. Good credit ratings with all my suppliers. Well trained staff. Plowed all my profits back into the business, growing it, ready to be there when every home had a video-disc player."

"And what happened?"

"DVDs." The man practically spat the word. "Freaky little things. Who'd have thought you could even fit a whole movie on such a little tiny thing? And what makes it better than a full-on laser disc? At least you can see the cover art on a laser disc."

The second man shrugged. "Sorry that—" He stopped short and was quiet for a long moment. Josh had paused to listen but didn't want to be caught staring, so he was about to move on when the man finally spoke. "Sorry, it's just . . . I was here, I guess, forty years ago.

Forty-two, I think it was. Not at this hotel, it didn't exist then, but downtown at the Lucky Strike. I met a woman at the blackjack tables, and we got on well, and next thing you know I was buying her dinner and, you know. We went out a few times, had a kind of a fling while I was in town. I haven't really thought much about her in the last decade or three, I guess. Just one of those things that happens when you're younger, and it's a pleasant memory but a vague one at best."

"What about her?" the first man asked, sounding confused. Josh was equally befuddled, and if the guy didn't get to the point, he was going to give up and go back to the Whirlwind.

"I could swear she just walked by," the man said. He seemed a little confused himself.

"Maybe she did. Maybe she never left Las Vegas."

"Yeah, maybe, but . . . well, if it's her, she hasn't aged a day since then. I mean, it was a long time ago, but she was a looker, you know, not the kind of girl you forget. I'd say maybe it's her daughter but there's no way a daughter would be an identical duplicate of her mother, is there? No, more likely it was someone who just sort of looks like her, and just being back in Vegas made me think it was her."

"That sounds right," the bitter man said. "Memory plays tricks. It's not a perfect storage device like a handy laser disc or anything, right?"

"Yeah," the guy said again. "Yeah, I guess so. But it's just weird, you know. Kind of creepy."

Josh was shaking his head, ready to get back to his last roll of quarters and block out the world's strangeness with the rush of the win and the noise of the machines, when he had a sudden insight that sent a chill down his spine. *A woman who didn't age in forty years? That could describe Season Howe.* Daniel Blessing hadn't aged in hundreds of years, and from everything he'd said about Season, the same went for her. The chances that it was Season were slim, he knew. More likely the man was as nuts as he sounded, or his memory was as bad as he said. Or the woman under discussion was some kind of female Dorian Gray, with a really heinous-looking portrait out in her garage.

But on the other hand, he knew from what Daniel had told them that Vegas would be just the kind of place Season might go to hide out. Full of transients, all the anonymity she could want. In Vegas people didn't ask too many questions; they didn't want to know a lot about anyone because they didn't want anyone to know a lot about them. If nothing else, Las Vegas was a good place to keep secrets.

Either way, he had to know. He hadn't seen the woman the old guy had been talking about, but he'd never forget what Season Howe looked like. The idea of trying to track her down by himself—even with thousands of people around—seemed absurdly dangerous. But no more so than letting her roam around his stomping grounds without knowing where she was. And Rebecca thought she had seen her once. Maybe Season was regretting having let them live, back in San Diego. *Besides,* he thought, his mind racing now as he tried to avoid surging panic, *if I find her, I can call the others, and maybe someone will have a good idea.*

He wasn't sure where to look, though. Since he hadn't been watching the man, but simply eavesdropping on what had seemed a fairly mundane conversation, he didn't know in which direction the man had been looking when she passed by. And the casino was not only crowded but, like all the big casinos, laid out in an intentionally chaotic fashion so that one couldn't walk a straight line but had to pass the maximum number of slots and gaming tables to get from one place to another.

The best Josh could do was pick a direction and strike out. If that didn't pay off, he'd work his way around and hope that he saw Season before she saw him. The worst thing would be if he couldn't find her, because then there was always the chance that she would find him. She had spared him once—spared all of them except Daniel, that day outside her San Diego hideout—but if she spotted him here and thought he was looking for her, he doubted that he'd get the same consideration again.

Josh had come to think of the casinos as a kind of refuge, where he could go to get sucked into the thrill of the game and forget his problems. He had forsaken most of his friends for them, with few regrets. But if Season was indeed loose here, his sanctuary was violated, his comfort zone suddenly a potential death trap.

Nearly frantic, he chose to go to the left,

and he dashed off in that direction, scanning the way ahead, dodging gamblers even as he cranked his head in every direction to eye those sitting at the machines he passed. He kept going that way until he reached one of the far walls, then peered through the windows as best he could into the restaurant there. Plenty of blondes, some very attractive, but no Season. He turned and went to his right, staying near the wall for a while, passing another restaurant, then struck out to his right again, cutting through another swath of casino.

He was afraid that he was calling attention to himself, darting this way and that, looking hard at every blond head he saw. He half expected security to snatch him up at any moment.

Still no sign of her. He tried to carve the casino into a regular pattern in his mind so he could make sure he covered all of it—notwithstanding the probability that she was not sitting still someplace, but was moving around just as much as he was, so he could miss her anyway—but its walkways were so irregular that that was hard to do.

Finally, Josh gave up. There was a plain-

clothes security agent giving him a hard eye—
he recognized the guy from other trips here,
and the man was always loitering, never playing, which marked him as an undercover man.
Josh hadn't seen Season anywhere. Probably his
first impression was the right one: Either the
old guy had been wrong altogether, or he had
seen someone who looked like his old flame,
but that someone was not Season Howe.

As he headed for the nearest exit, Josh felt
his heart rate start to calm, his breathing
become more regular. He had been, he realized
now, dangerously close to a full-fledged panic
attack. It had all been a false alarm, though. He
wouldn't be returning to this particular casino
for a while, but at least he didn't have to worry
about Season Howe.

He was almost out the door when he saw
her.

12

Scott didn't pace. It might almost have been better if he did. Instead, he sat down at the couch, turned on the TV, ran through the channels using the remote. Finding nothing of interest, he turned it off again, drummed his fingers on the couch, then rose and went to the kitchen, where he rummaged through the pantry. Again finding nothing, he went back to the couch, drummed for a while longer, then clicked the TV back on.

Brandy, sitting at the dining room table and trying to cram for a midterm, thought she would scream. Or kill him. Or kill him and then scream. Earlier, occasional trick-or-treaters had interrupted his agonized fidgeting, but their numbers had trickled and then they'd stopped coming altogether.

"Can you *please* try to control yourself?" she asked, impatience evident in her voice. She had given up trying to hide it.

"What? Am I bothering you?" *Clueless.*

"Brilliant deduction, Sherlock." She couldn't put a finger on precisely *when* she had stopped loving Scott. But this was the moment at which she became aware that she had, and it struck her hard, like a physical blow, and made her queasy, almost nauseous. She had, for a long time, loved the guy sitting there on the couch looking at her from behind his glasses like some lost little boy. But she didn't now. He had drifted away from her somehow. They had much in common, still— mutual friends, mutual interests—but that was a friendship, not a love affair or a lifetime commitment.

"It's just that I'm worried about her."

"About Kerry."

Scott nodded affirmation.

And there it is, Brandy thought. *The wedge that's come between us.*

"You think about her more than you do about me," she said simply. "About us."

He looked as surprised as if she'd slapped

him. His thin cheeks crimsoned. "That's not true. It's just . . ."

"It *is* true," Brandy said. "You can't get her off your mind. Since we came back from San Diego, you've talked about Kerry more than anything else. Your grades are slipping because you worry so much about her. You check e-mail, what, twenty times a day, just in case she's sent one? Thirty?"

"She's important. To us," Scott argued. He came off the couch now, walking toward her, and Brandy felt threatened by his approach. No, not threatened, that was wrong. Disturbed, though—she wanted distance. If he put his arms around her, held her close, if she breathed in the familiar scent of him, it would weaken her resolve. Somehow, this seemed important to her right now. Earlier, they'd taken turns answering the door to their apartment as trick-or-treaters came in search of candy, but since that had petered off they'd been alone with only the sounds of the TV and his finger-drumming disturbing the silence, grating on her nerves, pushing her toward a decision she had never wanted to make.

"She's important to you," Brandy shot

back. "Okay, to both of us. But only one of us is obsessed with her. One of us thinks she can take care of herself."

"Not against Season," Scott rejoined.

"We don't know that she's fighting Season," Brandy said. "In fact, we have every reason to believe that she's not, and that she's perfectly safe with Mother Blessing, like she told Rebecca."

"I wish she'd called here—," Scott began.

"Is that it? You're ticked that she talked to Rebecca instead of you? She said she tried here, didn't get an answer."

"We have voice mail," Scott pointed out defensively.

"Yeah, we do. And Rebecca said she was somehow talking via her computer, with no actual phone line. So maybe whatever magic made that work doesn't play well with voice mail. Maybe it wasn't even Kerry, maybe it was her audio doppelganger."

"It's just . . . I worry about her. I think she's up to something dangerous. I think she's the key to Season, somehow, and . . . I don't know." Instead of approaching Brandy, he flopped back down on the couch, as if he sensed the coldness with which she would have greeted his advance. It was almost as if she'd put up an invisible force field around herself, which was, in fact, what she had been trying to project. "Okay, yeah, you're right, I worry about her. She's our friend, is that a bad thing?"

"It is when it's to the exclusion of the rest of your life," Brandy offered. "Do you remember the last time you kissed me? I don't mean kissing back if I kiss you, but the last time you took the initiative? The last time you made love to me? The last time you even took my hand as we walked across campus? You've been so distracted, so—I have to say obsessed, again—with Kerry that you haven't been paying attention to anything or anyone else, including me. I've looked through your notebooks, Scott. Your notes are terrible. I don't think you're going to pass any of your classes. You can't live like this—or, I don't know, maybe you can, but I can't."

She paused, and Scott's gaze bored into her as if he were looking for the Brandy he'd once known behind this new, cruel mask. Finally, he spoke again. "What . . . what are you saying? It's . . . we're over? Is that it, Brandy? Because if it is, if you'd let what we have, what we've meant to each other, end because of . . . because of something like this, of me worrying about a mutual friend who's in trouble—she left her school, she went to some swamp—you know, that really sucks."

"Maybe it does." Brandy had to try hard not to shrug, but that would look too callous, even for her. "But it's her *Deliverance* fantasy; she's where she wants to be. You know, I'm sorry, Scott. This is not what I wanted at all. I wanted us to be together forever. But, see, by definition that requires both of us participating, and you haven't been. I don't see that changing. I think you love Kerry—or if not, your concern for Kerry outweighs every other aspect of your emotional life, which might as well be the same thing."

Finally, Scott seemed to understand what was happening, and anger clouded his face. She saw him looking at her, narrowed eyes twitching as if he were searching her face to see if she meant what she was saying. She was pretty sure that she did. At any rate, she'd said it—it was out there in the room now, like a tiger let out of a cage, and it couldn't be put back in.

She only hoped it didn't draw blood.

"Brandy, I . . ." Scott let the sentence hang, unfinished. He swallowed, and she thought she saw a tear forming at the corner of his eye. *At least that would be something,* she thought, *an emotional response that really was directed at me and not at Kerry.* But he sniffed once and rubbed his eyes with his knuckles, and when he blinked and looked her way again it was gone, if it had ever been there.

He looked like he was about to say something else when the phone rang. *This is a test,* she thought. *If he lunges for the phone, hoping it's Kerry or news of Kerry, then I'm right about this. If he understands that we're fighting for our own survival, as a couple, and lets it ring—*

He lunged. "Hello?"

He was quiet for a minute, his face growing ever more somber. "Okay," he said after a while. "Yeah, thanks. We'll be there."

He hung up the phone, left his place on the couch and came back into the kitchen. She didn't like the look on his face. "That was Josh," he said, and Brandy thought she detected a tremor in his voice. He opened the refrigerator and leaned inside, hunting for something, raising his voice so she could hear him. "He's found Season. We have to go to Las Vegas."

"What, right now?" Brandy asked, surprised. "We're kind of in the middle of something here. And Las Vegas is, like, two thousand miles away."

Scott swung around toward her, a Coke in his hand. "Brandy, you may not like it, but you're in this. You're part of this. Remember when Rebecca thought she saw her? If Season's in Las Vegas she might be hunting Josh—hunting all of us. Or she might just be trying to hide out. Either way, something's got to be done."

"What can we do?" she asked. She felt a sudden panic—she had hoped their Season-fighting days were far behind them, for the rest of their lives. "We can't hurt her. Even Daniel couldn't beat her."

"We can't just leave her alone," Scott insisted. "Josh could be in trouble. And if she's after him, she'll come for us, too. We have to try to do something. Rebecca's going to try to reach Kerry. Maybe with the help of Daniel's mother, she can . . ."

"Kerry's going to save the day?" Brandy

asked archly. "You just keep thinking that."

Scott threw his hands into the air. "Okay, whatever," he said. "I'm going to the airport to get the first flight to Vegas. You can come or not. Suit yourself. And anyway, *Deliverance* is hillbillies, not swamp rats." He headed into the bedroom, and a moment later Brandy heard the sounds of drawers being flung open, his closet ransacked, as he packed for the impromptu trip.

She only thought it over for a few minutes, listening to him prepare. She hadn't consciously changed her mind about loving him—almost as if a switch had been thrown, it was just over. He had demonstrated that his concerns were else-where, and that was all it took. The process, she was sure, had started a while ago; his obsession with Kerry had simply been the crucial card that brought all the others down.

But notwithstanding that, he was right. She was in this witch-hunt as much as he was, or as much as any of them with the possible excep-tion of Kerry. And even if she was no longer in love with Scott, she didn't want him to be injured. Maybe Kerry could take care of her-self, but Scott couldn't. Someone had to be there to keep an eye on him.

She went into the bedroom to gather the things she'd need. *I hope this is a short trip,* she thought anxiously. *I'm going to have to make up that midterm.*

"Samhain is a very special night," Mother Blessing explained. She was wearing a green, velvety robe, and while Kerry bathed in a specially scented tub, she had placed a similar robe on Kerry's bed. After Kerry donned the robe, marveling at its soft, luxurious fabric, they met in what had been the kitchen, except that, through some mystical process Kerry couldn't yet fathom, it had become a courtyard, open to the moon and the stars and an aromatic breeze off the Swamp.

The floor, once vinyl tiles, was now earthen. Candles flickered everywhere—short, fat ones on the bare ground; tall, narrow tapers in multitiered candelabra; tea lights in glass dishes or simply arranged in lines upon the stone altar that stood at one end of the impossible arena. When Mother Blessing had pushed the door open and motored into this place, Kerry hadn't believed her eyes. She tried surreptitiously to feel the ground with her hands, rolling dirt between her fingers to convince herself that it was real.

During her childhood, Halloween had been a very special event for Kerry—the one night she could really lose herself in imagination, in fantasy, giving herself permission to be someone else for the evening. She loved the costumes, the witches and jack-o'-lanterns and black cats, parties with bobbing for apples and other games, knocking on the doors of strangers and being rewarded for it with candy. She had never imagined a night like this one, though . . . had never believed that the witches were real.

"We celebrate the Old Ones on this night," Mother Blessing continued. "We thank them for the gifts they've given us this past year, and we ask them to bless the crops which are to be harvested." She allowed herself a chuckle. "Course, I don't do a lot of harvestin' myself, so that part's just kind of traditional. But still, someone's doin' it, and I use the crops plenty. Just don't pick 'em."

The Old Ones, Kerry knew from Mother Blessing's lectures, were the God and the Goddess. Mother Blessing had stressed that they were two facets of deity, and that other religions and cultures might see them differently—as a single deity, or as an entire pantheon full of gods and demigods. But in Mother Blessing's world, they were two: male and female, opposite sides of the coin. The God represented war, power, rationality, and the seed; the Goddess emotion, beauty, art, and the womb. "Sexist, ain't it?" she had said with a laugh. "But not really, because they're both all of those things. Or they contain all those things within them. Or their aspects can be seen in those things. It's a fluid system, child, that's the important part. However you want to think of it is the way it will work for you. It's only crucial that you do think of it, that you commune with them, because they *are* the power. You channel the power, nature provides the power, but they are part and parcel of the power."

"I think I understand," Kerry assured her. She was afraid of sounding simplistic, but it was a lot to take in and she was still processing. "I haven't done a lot of harvesting myself, but I'm sure happy there are fresh fruits and vegetables and grains."

"That's right," Mother Blessing said. She placed several objects on the altar: a cup, a bell, a knife. "Tonight is also a night of great power," she went on, her voice taking on a warning tone. "So our ritual must be cautious. We want to honor those who have passed, and to prepare for their eventual return. But we don't want to call them—on Samhain, that is far too easy to do and far too dangerous to contemplate."

"The dead can come back?" Kerry asked, hope sparking within her for a moment. Maybe there was a way to see Daniel again, to be with him . . .

"The dead always come back," Mother Blessing replied. "But not as those we remember. And not in frogs or rocks or, I expect, lawyers. Just as new people, with some trace fragments of who they were before buried deep inside them. But if they're summoned on Samhain and they're not ready to return . . . well, you don't want to know, do you?"

Actually, Kerry thought, *I kind of do.* But she decided she wouldn't let on about that. This whole thing was so exciting—finally being allowed to take part in a ritual, and such an important one at that. She felt that Mother Blessing was gradually learning to trust her. If she performed well here—which she figured meant keeping out of the way, not accidentally breaking anything, and doing whatever Mother Blessing asked of her—then surely Mother Blessing would ramp up her training, start in with the real goods. She knew it would be a long time before she could do the kinds of things that Daniel had, but baby steps were better than not walking at all.

Mother Blessing turned her cart around and was about to wheel away from the altar when a look of surprise washed over her face. She stopped cold and stared at the ground, as if listening intently to a voice Kerry couldn't hear. When she looked up again it was directly at Kerry. "Someone's trying to reach you."

Kerry said the first thing that popped into her mind. "The dead?"

"The living," Mother Blessing answered. "I hate to see our Samhain rites interrupted, but you had better see what they want. It's urgent."

"How . . . ?"

"Check your computer," Mother Blessing said. "You'll be able to get through. Tonight, magic is easy. The veils between worlds are thin. Go, child, go."

Kerry took a last look around at the unlikely courtyard, the candles, the objects arrayed on the altar, and herself and Mother Blessing in matching green robes. *I'll never learn this,* she thought angrily, *if I can't have some uninterrupted time to do it in.*

But she knew that Mother Blessing wouldn't send her away if there weren't a good reason. She went out through the door—into the rest of the house, just as if she'd been in the normal kitchen all along—and dashed down to her room. The laptop was in the cabinet next to her bed. As she booted up, she wondered what could possibly be so important.

13

Josh had figured he'd live his whole life without ever once saying—at least in any kind of serious way—the words "Follow that cab." But when he finally spotted Season at the Mandalay Bay, she was walking out the front door, and by the time Josh reached the door, a doorman was closing a taxi door behind her. Josh had jumped into the next cab in line and uttered those eternal words, and as the taxi pulled out into the street, he was glad he hadn't gambled away the second roll of quarters in his pocket.

Both cabs rolled out onto Las Vegas Boulevard—the Strip—and were immediately stuck in gridlock. The Strip was thick with vehicles: huge stretch limos, SUVs, hotel shuttles, and cabs mixing with normal passenger cars and the occasional city bus in a ballet of steel, glass, and rubber performed to a soundtrack of honking horns, screeching brakes, and squealing tires. Josh was half afraid that his cab would accidentally catch up to or pass the one Season rode in, and that either she'd see him or his driver would misunderstand the nature of the request and, thinking he was trying to join her, would flag the other driver down or radio him.

As it turned out, though, that didn't happen. Season's cab stayed ahead of theirs, turning off the Strip at Flamingo and cutting down to the Maryland Parkway, which ran parallel to Las Vegas Boulevard but without as much traffic. Josh watched the dollars mount up on the taxi's meter as the car swallowed up the miles toward downtown. He knew he should call the rest of the summer gang, but he didn't want the cabbie to hear what he had to say; bad enough that by not having a destination, but asking the driver to follow another car, he was creating a memory that would stick with the guy.

Finally, the other cab stopped at a motel near downtown, the Come-On Inn. It was nothing special—not the kind of place Josh would have expected Season to stay. But then again, he thought, if privacy was her primary consideration, the big casinos probably weren't ideal. They had cameras everywhere, they had staff who tried to remember the guests, especially regulars. At this place one could probably get a room without even showing identification, and the staff most likely made a point of not prying into a guest's affairs.

Josh glanced at the meter again. Thirteen bucks, and still climbing. He had just the quarter roll and a couple of dollar bills on him. "Stop here," he said. He reached into his pocket, pulled out the paper roll of quarters, and split it with his hand. When the driver reached around to collect, Josh punched the roll toward him, spraying him with change. "Sorry!" Josh shouted. He grabbed the door handle, opened it and darted from the cab while the driver struggled with the coins.

The guy shouted at him, but Josh ran into the shadows behind a vacant commercial building. He stayed there for a few minutes, breathing hard, his heart pounding, while the cab circled the block. Josh felt terrible—he hated to rip off an honest cab driver just trying to make a living—but this was an emergency situation. As it was, he'd been left with just a few quarters of his own, and the two bills. *Damn Whirlwind,* he thought.

When the coast was clear, Josh emerged from the shadows, just in time to see an upstairs door close behind Season. He moved a little closer until he could see the number on it: 17. Behind heavy drapes, a light turned on. It looked as if she was alone in the room, and, he hoped, in there for the night.

Now he dug out his cell phone, scrolled through his saved numbers, and dialed Rebecca. "Happy Halloween," she answered cheerfully.

"Beck? It's Josh."

"Hi Josh, how are you?"

"Listen, Rebecca, this isn't a social call. It's Season. I found her."

There was a long silence from the other end. When Rebecca spoke again, there was a tremor in her voice, and Josh felt sorry for having to put her through this. "If this is a Halloween prank, Josh, it's not a very funny one."

"It's not a joke, Beck. She's here, in Vegas. I

just tailed her to her hotel. We have to do something."

"What can we do, Josh? You're better off getting out of there before she sees you."

"But . . . Rebecca, she's not going to stop being a threat. To us and to others. Don't you think we should try to fight her while we have the advantage?"

"What advantage is that? She has all the power."

"We have surprise," Josh countered, hoping he didn't sound as foolishly desperate as he felt.

"We had that before, too. And we also had Daniel. Look at where it got him."

"Yeah, but she was ready for Daniel. She knew he was around, knew she'd be facing him sometime. She doesn't know that we know where she is."

"Because she's not worried about us, because we can't do a thing to her," Rebecca pointed out. "We're powerless against her, Josh. Get out of there while you can."

"Maybe we're not so powerless after all, Beck," he argued. "Didn't you say that Kerry was learning magic from Mother Blessing? Maybe there's something she can do."

Another pause from Rebecca. Her hesitation surprised him. Sure, it was stupid to think they had any chance against Season. But it was suicidal to just leave her roaming freely around his town. "Maybe," she said at last. "Are you sure she hasn't seen you?"

"I'm sure." Josh realized that another advantage of this crummy motel was that in any of the big hotels, security would have thrown him off the premises before too long. Here, though, he should be able to keep an eye on her door at all times. "Can you try to get through to Kerry? I'll call Scott and Brandy. I'm sure if we all get together we can think of something. But it's got to be fast—I don't want to lose her again."

Rebecca sighed loudly enough that he wasn't sure he needed the phone to hear it. "Okay," she said. "I'll reach Kerry, somehow, and then I'll catch the first plane out there. I'll call you when I get there, and you can tell me where you are."

"That's great, Rebecca. Thanks. I really think this is important."

After he disconnected the call he tried to figure out why he thought that. She was right, of course. They had no way to mount a successful offense against Season Howe. Unless, that is, Kerry had learned some really impressive magic in the weeks she'd been gone. Even so, the chance that in such a brief period of training she had picked up any skills that Daniel hadn't acquired after hundreds of years was worse than slim.

But really, he thought, *that doesn't matter. Daniel died. Mace died. Others will die. Now that we have a lead on her, we have to play it out, no matter what. To turn our backs on her would be the only unforgivable thing.*

He scrolled down to Scott and Brandy's number and pushed send.

With every passing day in the Great Dismal, Kerry felt more comfortable there—so much so that when she had to leave, she was surprised by a pang of regret, as if she were leaving a home she'd known for years. She bade Mother Blessing goodbye before first light, having missed the whole Samhain observance, which the older woman had said had had to go on as scheduled before midnight changed the date. After the ritual was over, Mother Blessing had called her back into the kitchen, which was, once again, just a kitchen, and they had sat down together at the table with glasses of milk and a plate of cookies between them.

"Y'all have to go," Mother Blessing had said.

Kerry had come to the same conclusion, but she had expected to have to convince Mother Blessing. That the witch herself suggested it came as a surprise. "I know," she agreed. "I'm just not sure what I can do."

"You'll do whatever you can. The woman is just evil. You know why she was at a casino instead of celebrating Samhain like she should've been? She thinks she's nontraditional, but it's the tradition that is so important to the craft. She just likes to do things her own way, no matter what." Kerry could tell from Mother Blessing's tone, and the sneer on her lips, that this was an enormous sin in her eyes. "I want y'all to understand why it's so important that Season Howe be stopped," Mother Blessing continued. "And sooner better than later."

"Well, to start with, she's a killer, right?" Kerry offered.

"She is that, true," Mother Blessing said. "More urgently, though, did Daniel ever tell y'all about the Witches' Convocation?"

"Yes, he mentioned it." Every five hundred years all the world's witches gathered for a festival, a sharing of information, and a combination social and business gathering. Kerry remembered, with a pain in her chest like a spike to the heart, that he had been looking forward to his first one.

"Well," Mother Blessing went on, "this one's the first since Season destroyed Slocumb. I'm fixing to bring charges against her for it. But word is she's got a counterattack planned—that she's thinkin' she'll demand sanctions against us for chasin' after her for so long, and she'll use that as a forum to deflect blame for Slocumb onto someone else. Maybe even me."

Kerry was astonished to hear this. "Could she get away with that?"

Mother Blessing tucked a cookie neatly into her mouth and chewed while nodding. "It's all political," she said when she had swallowed it. "If she could sway enough votes to her side, she could pull it off."

"What would the sanctions be?" Kerry wanted to know.

Now Mother Blessing shrugged. "Could be just about anything. I might have to give up magic until the next Convocation. I might have to pay a fine of some kind. Could be I'd even have to pay with my life."

Kerry had been about to sip some milk, but now she put the glass down hard. "You're kidding."

"I wouldn't joke about something like that, would I, child?"

"I guess not. It just seems sort of extreme."

Another shrug. "If her accusations were true, it might be a fair judgment. Since they're not, though, I have to keep her from bringin' 'em if I can. Be better to stop her before she ever makes it to the Convocation so I don't have to worry about tryin' to outmaneuver her once we're there."

After sorting through the logistics of how to get to Vegas from the Swamp, Kerry had turned in for a few hours of restless sleep. As soon as the morning light filtered through the trees into the swamp, she was in Mother Blessing's skiff, rowing for the old Slocumb site, where her van still waited. By the time she reached it her arms and shoulders were sore from the workout, and she was covered with a film of sweat in spite of the cool of the morning. She hiked across the wasted, barren land with a deeper appreciation for what had occurred there than she'd had before reading Daniel's account of that catastrophic day. When she reached her minivan she thought for a moment that she saw shadows slipping away from it into the reeds. She wasn't entirely sure, but it wouldn't have surprised her to know that Mother Blessing had sent simulacra to guard it until her return.

The van started right up. Sitting behind the wheel felt oddly foreign to her, as if hiking through the swamp had already become her everyday life, and the world of cars and roads and cities a kind of half-remembered dream. But she hadn't forgotten how to drive, so she put the vehicle into gear, turned it around and headed back toward the highway, back toward Norfolk and an airport from which she could fly to Las Vegas.

Season was there. She wasn't sure what she'd do to Season—Mother Blessing had armed her with some potent spells, though she'd had no time to practice them—but that would come. The important thing was finding her again. Confronting her.

Making sure she paid for what she did to Daniel. And making sure she would never make it to the Witches' Convocation, where she might compound her crimes by blaming them on Mother Blessing.

Kerry's resolve was tempered steel. The Bulldog was back.

14

Josh spent the night huddled in the doorway of the vacant building, drawing his coat around him for whatever warmth it could offer, smoking for the same reason, wishing he had a car he could sit in or a credit card so he could take a room at the Come-On Inn for himself. Las Vegas was a desert city, which meant that on summer days the sun could be merciless, but on October-melting-into-November nights, the same lack of cloud cover that let the sun beat down during the day allowed the city's heat to be quickly dissipated. The result was nights that felt positively arctic, at least by Josh's standards. He figured frostbite was not a genuine concern, but he'd spent more comfortable nights, and he couldn't think of many worse.

Finally, though, the sun did reappear above the eastern horizon, and with its glow the city began to awaken. Parts of it, of course, never slept—the casinos were open 24/7—but most of the city, away from the bright lights and high rollers, operated on a more traditional schedule. As the sun warmed the air, birds began to chirp their morning songs, cars and buses emerged onto the streets, and Josh felt his bones start to thaw.

He also realized another downside to his plan. His stomach woke up too, and it began churning hungrily. He'd hardly slept, he'd had nothing to eat or drink, and he'd been smoking like a chimney. He needed to eat something now, and have some water, or he'd be sick. But there was nothing he could see within immediate range, no handy market or diner, and if he went looking for something he could buy or steal he'd run the risk of missing Season, should she emerge from her hidey-hole. He wondered what Philip Marlowe would do in this situation, or Mike Hammer. Fictional private eyes didn't need to eat as regularly as real people, he decided, so they'd probably just buck it up, maybe knock back a shot of whiskey, and continue the surveillance. Sooner or later someone would knock them out, and then they'd have the opportunity to grab a few winks and maybe a sandwich.

The sound of his cell phone's electronic tune startled him. He fished it from his pocket with a shaking hand. "Yeah?"

"Hi, Josh." Rebecca Levine. She sounded close, but that was meaningless these days, he knew. It had more to do with how strong the cell signal was at any given spot than where someone was in relation to the caller.

"Beck, hey. Where are you?"

"At the airport," she said.

"McCarran?"

"Here in Las Vegas."

He moved the phone from his ear long enough to check the time. Seven-fifteen. "Listen," he said, regretting the words even before he spoke them. "I think our bird's gonna stay in her cage a while longer. Why don't you rent a car, but then stay at the airport a while? Brandy and Scott are supposed to get here at 10:12. You might as well wait and bring them when you come."

"I talked to Kerry last night," Rebecca

reported. "She'll be here this morning too."

"That's great," Josh said. "I'm glad you were able to reach her."

"Is everything okay?"

"I could use some grub," Josh admitted. "And I'm sure I need a shower. But I'm fine, I guess. No movement from Season after she went into her room last night."

"It's so amazing that you found her," Rebecca said. Josh thought he caught a hint of disbelief in her voice, as if Rebecca questioned whether it was, in fact, simply coincidence that put Josh and Season in the same building at the same time. Josh didn't know how to answer that, because he'd had the same concern himself.

If it's not coincidence, then we could be playing right into her hands.

That idea chilled him to his core. But in fact, he remembered, Rebecca had seen her first—or had thought she had. Which didn't mean this wasn't a trap of some kind. In fact, the more he dwelled on it, the more it seemed to confirm that idea. "Yeah," he said simply. "I don't know what we're going to do now, but at least we've got her pinned down."

"I think Kerry will have some ideas," Rebecca offered.

"She'd better. I sure don't."

"She will." Rebecca sounded more like someone trying to project confidence than someone who actually felt it, but Josh was willing to take what he could get. "You've got my number, so if anything comes up, give me a call, okay?"

"Absolutely," Josh assured her. The fact was, as much as he liked Rebecca, he could think of no one less useful for surveillance or combat, if it came to that. Her manner of dress tended toward flowing skirts and tie-dye, which would make her stand out in a crowd or in a casino— not that Josh didn't, in his Goth blacks and jet hair. But at least during the night his chosen wardrobe had helped him blend into the shadows. Then there was the fact that Rebecca was just about the most peaceful soul he'd ever known. He was vegan, but even so, he was willing to swat a hungry mosquito. Rebecca would argue for the creature's life, then extend her arm to it. She had needed to be informed of Season's reappearance because she was part of the original group that had faced the witch during the summer, but keeping her at the airport, taking care of logistical things like renting a car, was the best use for her.

Still, he thought as he squirmed in the doorway, *I could have had her pick up some granola or something.*

Two more hours had passed when the door to Room 17 opened. Josh looked around anxiously, hoping to spot a cab. If she was going somewhere by car, or had a ride coming, he was out of luck. This was what he had hoped wouldn't happen until Rebecca showed up with the others in her rental. He watched Season step outside onto the walkway that ran past all the second-floor doors, her honey-blond hair catching the morning sun. She wore what looked like a brown leather suit, snug pants and a jeans-style jacket with a white shirt underneath it. Josh pressed himself back against the door, as deep in shadow as he could get, while she slowly surveyed the neighborhood.

Instead of getting into a car, though, Season descended the staircase and walked across the street to a bus stop. Almost no one used public transportation in Vegas, Josh knew, except those so economically disadvantaged that they just couldn't afford a car. Which was probably precisely why Season was using it—if she were hiding out she'd want to vary her routine, not be predictable. Cab last night, bus this morning. Made perfect sense.

But that didn't solve his predicament. He had an idea that might, though. So far, no bus was in sight. Bus stops weren't too terribly spread out around this neighborhood. He had an opportunity, then, if he hurried, to reach the next bus stop down the line, and to get on the bus before Season did. Of course, that came with a couple of pitfalls, too. If he missed the bus he'd lose Season. If she changed her mind and didn't take the bus, or crossed the street and hopped one going in another direction, he was screwed. And if she recognized him once she got on, she'd ... well, it didn't help to dwell on such things. It was a gamble, but Josh was a gambler. He ran.

He went around behind the building next to which he'd spent the night, knowing as he did that letting Season out of his sight only decreased the odds in his favor. But if she saw him running, her guard would certainly be raised. This way she'd only have a brief glimpse of him, if at all, when he ran across the distant intersection more than a block away from the one where she waited at the bus stop. Josh put aside his exhaustion, his hunger, and his fear, and sprinted full out. Two blocks beyond Season's location, he cut back over to the street she was on.

From here, he looked in both directions, spotting a bus stop one more block away. He started for it at the same time that a city bus swung around the corner, coming toward him. He had been running with everything he had—he was not, he'd readily admit, exactly track-star material—but now he reached deep down inside, knowing he had to find a little more speed, a little more endurance, if he hoped to beat the smoke-belching vehicle. Feet pounding pavement, head jarring with every step, aching lungs sucking air, he ran, finally reaching the bus stop just as the bus lurched to the curb.

The driver looked curiously at him as he boarded, but it was all Josh could do to drop his fare into the slot and request a transfer. Trying to catch his breath, he moved toward the back of the bus. He spotted an open window seat next to a wrinkled Latino man with a steel lunchbox on his lap, and ignored several empty seats to take that one, to eliminate the chance that Season might sit next to him. The man frowned, but relented and allowed Josh to squeeze past him.

When the bus rumbled up to the next stop, Josh scrunched down in the seat as far as he could, just looking over the seat back in front of him from the tops of his eyes. For a terrible moment he feared that Season had changed her mind, that she wasn't getting on after all, and that he would be taking a bus ride to nowhere while she slipped away. But then her familiar features showed up in the doorway, another ray of light striking her—as if illuminated by an admiring sun—just before she came into the bus's shadow. She didn't even glance his way, but took an available seat near the front.

The horrible thought struck him, once again, that this was not in fact Season Howe, but simply some innocent young woman who happened to resemble her. *Wouldn't Season sense me sitting here?* he wondered. *Wouldn't she just know?*

But when he saw her run her fingers through her hair or glance toward the back of the bus, he knew again that it was indeed Season. At those moments he quickly looked away, lest the old "I know someone is watching me" radar kick in and alert her to his presence.

Josh's next challenge came when she got off the bus, just outside the New York–New York casino. Should he stay on until the next stop and risk losing her in the crowd? Or get off here and risk being seen? He decided that being seen was the lesser of the two worries, since there were so many people in the casino and so many places she might go. He stayed in his seat until she was off the bus, then he rose, pushed past lunchbox guy, and darted for the back door. By the time he made it off, she was already headed toward the casino's entrance.

He tore his cell from his pocket, breathlessly punched Rebecca's number. When she answered, he said, "Beck, she's at New York. Where are you?"

"Kerry's just shown up," Rebecca answered. "We'll be there in a few minutes."

"Okay," he said. "Take Tropicana to the Strip and turn right."

"I've been memorizing the map," she assured him. "We'll be right there. Don't do anything stupid."

Sprinting for the door, he broke the connection. By any reasonable definition, this whole thing was stupid. The fact that Season Howe was entering a small-scale reproduction of New York City—complete with Statue of Liberty, Times Square, and fireboats in the harbor—was absurd.

But that was Vegas.

Inside, she had already blended in with the rest of the crowd: tourists, gamblers, employees, and sightseers gawking at the replica Big Apple that filled the huge building. Josh tried to slow his pace, not wanting to appear frantic or to chance missing her if she'd simply stepped behind something or someone. She was inside now—it'd be a while before she made it back out. He'd find her.

By the time he did, though, panic had almost overtaken him. He felt like the casino was as crowded as the real New York, like there were nine million people in the place and he was only looking for one. He eventually spotted her, though, sitting at a hundred-dollar-minimum blackjack table, looking as at home as if she owned the place. This, he realized, was probably a great way for a witch to generate cash flow: A few magically altered cards at the right moment could keep her in the green for a long time, and the pit bosses would never be able to figure out how she was cheating. Josh felt a moment's envy—this was the kind of action he craved but could never afford. Maybe if he'd been in league with Season instead of with the good guys, he'd be sitting next to her instead of wearing the same stinking clothes he'd had on all night, ragged and hungry and beyond exhausted.

He had made his choices, though. He hung back and watched her play, the pile of chips before her growing steadily. After a little while, he realized he wasn't the only one watching her. From a bank of slots nearby, two men glared at her with eerie yellow eyes. There was something not right about them, he noticed. When they started to move it became even more apparent. They weren't men at all; he could see bits of casino debris stuck to them— no, stuck *in* them, as if it were part of them— cigarette butts and change cups, plastic and paper coin rolls. These were manufactured men—Josh searched his memory for the term Daniel Blessing had used. *Simulacra.* It came to him just as they headed for her. She hadn't seen them yet, and he knew that if she did, it would spook her—no way would she still be around when Kerry and the others showed up. He was sure the simulacra couldn't defeat her alone; if they'd been able to, Daniel's quest would have ended ages before.

He was also pretty sure that Kerry and the gang wouldn't be able to beat her either. But if she was hunting them down, then they had to at least try. And he didn't know what tricks Mother Blessing might have outfitted Kerry with. No matter what, he had to keep the simulacra from scaring off Season before Kerry arrived.

He did the only thing he could think of. He moved in front of them, putting his hands out to stop them. "Wait," he said urgently, trying to keep his voice low so as not to attract casino security. "I know what you are. You work for Mother Blessing, right?"

The two barely spared him a glance. He could see that he was right, though; there was nothing natural about these creatures. *Men* was the wrong word for them. They ignored his entreaties, as if deaf to him. One of them swept an arm sideways, catching Josh in the chest and hurling him into the slot machines. Pain shot through his back and flashes of light filled his vision. But he forced himself to his feet again, and dashed toward the creatures, knowing even as he did so that it was too late now to prevent a scene. His gambler's instincts, though, told him that if the simulacra got to Season first, he'd never get another shot at her, and he wasn't willing to let that happen. "Stop!" he called. "You'll blow everything."

This time one of the simulacra turned toward him. Its face was featureless but its body language spoke volumes, and Josh got the sense that it would not interrupt its mission for anything. The thing snatched up a stool from in front of a video poker machine, tearing it loose from its moorings, and drove its jagged base into Josh's chest. Fire lanced into him, obscuring the comparatively minor pain he'd felt before. This was like nothing he'd ever experienced: The whole world was turning dark, except for the white-hot bolt of agony at his chest.

Josh felt himself slumping backward, falling to the floor. The world moved before him in slow motion. The simulacra, having forgotten him, advanced on Season. She came up from her seat, her pretty face set with a determined scowl, sparing only a glance for Josh before she faced the two not-men. All around, people went into slo-mo action, like something from a Peckinpah battle sequence: civilians ducking for cover, security forces converging on the scene. Josh heard screams, but distantly, as if through some kind of filter.

One of the simulacra overturned a craps table as it rushed toward her. Chips spun everywhere, arcing through the air like rainbows. Again, voices were raised, but they sounded to Josh like deep bellows, like foghorns on faraway shores, and when the table hit the ground, the crash came to him slowly, as if he were underwater.

But then Season went into action, and it was a beautiful thing to behold: practiced, efficient, without a wasted motion. She spoke words Josh couldn't hear, inscribed gestures in the air that his eyes couldn't track. Bursts of glowing energy pulsed from her upraised hands. The simulacra halted in their tracks, caught in beams of light that pummeled them like hurricane winds. They tried to push forward against her magical field, but it tore at them, tattering their makeshift clothing, keeping them at bay. Now they both howled their anguish, and this Josh could hear even over the dull rush that filled his ears: long, drawn-out screams as they began to disassemble. Pieces of trash, a mannequin's arm, a hunk of partially shredded black tire, strips of wire—Josh saw them all come into focus as they tore away from the simulacra's bodies under Season's steady assault. The image was fascinating and terrible at the same time—nonliving beings dismantling bit by bit—and Josh couldn't help being impressed by Season's bold stance as she stood there, unshaken by their attack, unmoved by the commotion around her, until her task was done.

Finally it was.

The simulacra gone, Season shook off the meaty hands of the security officers who tried to grab her and headed straight for Josh. She swam in and out of focus as she neared. Josh was cold, so cold, but at least his chest had stopped hurting, and that was something. He started to think that maybe he'd survive this after all, until he saw Season bearing down on him. His eyes fluttered closed; he fought them open again, and she was nearer.

The expression on her face as she knelt before him was the scariest thing he'd seen yet. It was concerned, almost tender—her clear blue eyes wide, moist lips parted—but at the same time utterly without hope. Her words confirmed this impression. "It's too late for me to help you," she said softly. "But thank you for what you did. Maybe this will help."

She touched his cheek, fingers as gentle as a whisper, and spoke a single word. Instantly, all the pain faded away. The cold vanished. Josh felt as comfortable as he ever had in his life. He was dying. He had known that, but where moments before he had been in utter agony, now he felt at peace with it. That was Season's gift to him, and it was not one he could take lightly.

He touched his chest, feeling the tacky blood that flowed there, soaking his clothing and skin. In the dim distance he saw Season running, twirling like a quarterback to elude the security forces trying to tackle her. He couldn't help thinking that they had all misjudged her, and he knew they were coming, Kerry and the rest, and had to be told. He just had to hang on long enough to let them know. Or he had to send them a message some other way.

He tried to free his cell phone from his pocket but it slipped from his wet hands and clattered away. He didn't have the strength to lift it anyway, he was sure. Dipping his finger in his own blood, Josh Quinn began to write on the side of a slot machine.

15

When Kerry came down the escalator into the central baggage-claim area of Las Vegas's McCarran Airport, Rebecca, Scott, and Brandy were waiting for her, Rebecca holding a big, hastily lettered sign that said "Bulldog Profitt." Kerry began to laugh immediately, the first good, long belly laugh she'd had in a long time. The others surrounded her and enmeshed her into a textbook-quality group hug that lasted until the laughter faded and the import of the trip began to settle among them again.

As Rebecca directed them to the parking structure where the rental car waited, Scott inclined his head toward a young woman dressed in a skimpy showgirl's outfit, complete with feathered headgear, holding a sign welcoming visitors to the resort she repre-sented. Then he pointed at the double rank of slot machines filling the center of the baggage-claim area. "No wonder Season likes this place," he said lightly. "It's like a surrealist's bad dream. No one would even notice her here."

Rebecca, resplendent in a long broomstick skirt and an embroidered denim top, nodded her head. "I read someplace that more fugitives from justice pick Las Vegas to hide out in than any other city."

"I believe that," Brandy chimed in. She looked stylish as ever in a peach-colored, long-sleeve thermal top with low-rise twill pants and black Paul Frank sneakers, and she tossed Kerry a smile like they were long-lost sisters. "After all, Josh lives here."

"He likes crime stories," Scott countered. "I don't think he's so big on actual crime."

"I'm just saying," Brandy shot back. "The spoon doesn't fall far from the kettle, or some-thing like that."

Rebecca cracked up again. "That doesn't even make any sense," she said, her face turn-ing red.

"It's Josh we're talking about," Brandy reminded her. "Who said making sense entered into it?"

The banter continued until they were in the car and Rebecca, after giving them a brief update on her last conversation with Josh, focused on driving. Scott and Brandy sat in back, hushed, while Kerry watched out the windows.

Emergency vehicles overtook them on the short trip from the airport—police cars, fire trucks, ambulances, lights flashing, sirens blaring. Traffic already jammed Las Vegas Boulevard, but somehow the cars on the street managed to pull to the sides, and the official vehicles wove through. Kerry wrinkled her forehead. "I've got a bad feeling about this," she said. "Hurry up, Beck."

Rebecca nodded grimly and pulled out, beating most of the other cars back into the lane after the emergency vehicles had passed through. "I'm on it," she said, flooring the accelerator. The rented Maxima lunged forward. Kerry was impressed by the way Rebecca handled the car. Ignoring the complaining horns, she muscled it from one lane to the next, pushing her way through before traffic had a chance to jam up again.

Within minutes, New York's skyline, or an approximation of it wrapped by a roller coaster, loomed on the left. Rebecca turned into the self-parking structure and the four of them ran from the car into the casino, Rebecca trying furiously to reach Josh on his cell phone. It rang and rang, she reported, but he did not answer. Kerry swallowed hard, expecting the worst.

Inside, the worst was what they found. Uniformed police officers were shooing away gamblers and onlookers, trying to spread yellow crime-scene tape across a wide swath of the casino floor. People stood around with stunned looks on their faces, some in tears, some strangely excited, as if they'd just seen a show put on by the establishment and felt they'd gotten their money's worth. Kerry shoved her way through the clot of people, craning her head to see around the cops, EMTs, and firefighters. The first thing she noticed was a strange assortment of trash strewn around the floor—the wheel of a shopping cart, a paper cup from an overpriced coffee shop, some general casino litter. Anyone else looking at the random junk would have wondered why it was all there, but to Kerry there was only one possible answer: simulacra had been here. She'd told Mother Blessing she was going to Las Vegas to investigate a Season sighting; the old witch must have sent her own scouts ahead.

But then her eyes rested on another sight, one that chilled her to the core, as if she'd just taken a cold shower inside a deep freeze.

Josh—or rather, a crumpled shape that had once been Josh, had once contained the essence of him—was splayed against a bank of slot machines. In the center of his chest a hole gaped, red and meaty, and blood from it had poured down his torn shirt, pooling on the ground between his legs.

Next to him, on the side of one of the slots, were four letters, scrawled in blood by a shaky hand.

SEAS

As if there were any doubt, Kerry thought. "Leave it to Josh," she said quietly to Scott, who had come up beside her. She pointed to the writing. "He fingered his own killer."

"Just like something out of one of those hard-boiled movies he loves," Scott answered. His voice broke when he said it, and Kerry knew he was close to tears. That was okay.

So was she.

Kerry Profitt's diary, November 1.

We couldn't stay at NY-NY—couldn't bring ourselves to—so we're across the street at the MGM Grand. It's my first time here, and I'd like to think there's something grand about it, but the fact is that we are all just staying the night because we're too drained to actually make any moves toward going home.

Three down:

Mace Winston.

Daniel Blessing.

Josh Quinn.

Pausing to look at my friends. . .

Scott Banner sits in a chair, staring out the window. Brandy Pearson's reading a textbook she brought with her, sitting on the bed with her legs folded beneath her, making herself as small as possible. Something's wrong there—trouble between those two, though neither one has said a word about it. Neither has said much of anything, come to think of it, since we saw Josh. They asked me a couple of questions about Mother Blessing and the Swamp, I asked them a few about school and their lives. I don't think any of us heard the answers. But I don't think Scott and Brandy have touched each other once since I got here, if you don't count that group hug. Rebecca Levine, beautiful flower child, has barely stopped weeping since we saw Josh's body. Now she stares vacantly at the TV, watching a moronic reality show with the sound turned so low I can barely hear it. Which is fine with me.

Rebecca also told me something apparently everyone else has known for some time now—that she thought she saw Season at some bogus séance. Which maybe wasn't as bogus as she thought. Maybe Season has been hunting us down, one by one.

So I can't help wondering: Which one is next? Season has taken three friends from me so far. Not just from me, from the world. Three flames snuffed, three lights extinguished. Three people who could have changed the world. Would Mace have discovered a cure for cancer? Not likely, I guess. But he might have coached a baseball team and befriended a sad, fatherless boy, and isn't that just as valuable an accomplishment? Josh might never have composed a stirring symphony but he might have skipped through a park on a sunny spring day, bringing smiles to the faces of everyone who saw him. Daniel . . .

Daniel saved lives, dedicated himself to bringing Season Howe to justice, and still found time to love me. To change my life, to pull me out of my own self-obsessed rut and give me some kind of direction, a goal, a desire to affect something larger than just myself.

We can never measure the impact we have on others, never know when a friendly word to a cashier at the market or a smile bestowed on a stranger or a few bucks to a charity might strike at just the right time to make someone's day, or give someone hope, or lend the tools someone needs to rebuild something that's broken. And so we can never know which life, cut short, might be one that the world needed. Since it's unlikely that Josh, Mace, or Daniel would have eventually become supervillains or anything, the loss of these lives, the tragedy of their early endings, is that their gifts, whatever they were to be, will never be realized. Okay, I guess it's hard to apply that to three-hundred-year-old Daniel, but still, he seemed young to me, and he had an important task that was left unfinished.

Not that their lives were wasted. They gave to me, to the others in this room, to their families, and to strangers. Rebecca wanted us to go see Josh's mother, but the rest of us talked her out of that—

considering what we've found ourselves mixed up in, we've all agreed to keep parents, family, and friends out of the loop. Safer for them, safer for us. I'm sure Josh never told his mom anything about us, and if we had shown up with our crazy stories, it would have just made a hard day even worse.

We don't know if Season is still in Vegas. Rebecca was the last one to talk to Josh, but he never told her where he staked Season out last night, so we don't even know where she was staying. Chances are, though, given that she battled simulacra, she knows her cover here is blown and she's already on the move. By plane, car, train, bus? Don't know.

I leave in the morning, back to Virginia, back to the Great Dismal. So do the others, Brandy and Scott for Harvard, Rebecca for UC Santa Cruz. My college pals, and me, witchy apprentice girl.

I don't know what they're all learning. But I know what my major is, what my course of study has to be. Intense, comprehensive, accelerated.

How to kill Season Howe.

More later.

K.

16

The sky over the Great Dismal Swamp was heavy and gray, lowering overhead like a leaden shroud, which suited Kerry's mood just fine. She had parked the minivan in its usual spot and rowed back through the ever-more-familiar Swamp to Mother Blessing's ramshackle cabin/comfortable suburban home (depending on whether one was outside or in). Kerry thought she felt eyes tracking her the whole way, but whether it was simulacra or snakes, birds, and other swamp wildlife, she couldn't have said.

Mother Blessing met her with a bottle of Coke and a tray of ham sandwiches on Wonder bread, and they sat together in the kitchen while Kerry filled her in on what had happened. The older woman was sympathetic, listening attentively until Kerry declared that she was exhausted and needed to get some sleep. Mother Blessing patted Kerry's arm. "Y'all get a good night's sleep, child. Tomorrow'll be a busy day."

"Busy with what?" Kerry asked, stifling a yawn. She had hardly slept at all the night before; images of Josh and Daniel filled her head. Though she'd dozed a little on the flight home, she really was weary to the bone.

"Well, it's time you learned some serious magic, isn't it?" Mother Blessing said. "Someone's got to stand up to Season, and I guess it might just as well be you."

"Are you sure I can do that?" Kerry asked excitedly. She wanted it more than anything, but she had thought she'd have to persuade Mother Blessing. Now she was almost afraid that the witch had made the promise in hopes that Kerry would realize she was asking too much and back off. She almost wished Mother Blessing had waited until the morning to make this announcement—now, tired as she was, she feared she'd have a hard time sleeping. Everything she'd been shown so far had been basic stuff, some beginner's tricks and a bunch of theory. But she had seen Daniel and Season at work, knew there was far more to be learned.

Mother Blessing nodded gravely. "I reckon we'll find out, Kerry," she said. "Tomorrow. Y'all get to bed now."

Kerry did as she was told, and to her surprise, as soon as she put her head on the pillow, she felt consciousness fading away. Tragedy and possibility whirled around in her mind, each feeding on the other, but soon enough they both emptied into nothingness and she slept.

"Most magical systems won't let one practitioner do harm to another," Mother Blessing explained the next day. They were back in the kitchen, which seemed to be where the woman spent most of her time, day and night. Kerry sat at the table in a heavy cable-knit sweater and soft, forest-green fleece pants, her long dark hair tugged into a tight ponytail. Dressed in her usual stretch polyesters under a shapeless housecoat, Mother Blessing rode her scooter, rolling it this way and that like a lecturer pacing while she spoke. "Violence is limited, in those systems, to the evil, the outlaws or renegades. Black magicians who call up destructive demons, for instance, are hated by white magicians. If Wiccans knew half of what they could do by simply taking their studies a few steps further, applying their powers in different ways, their little flowered headpieces would most likely melt off them." She had a small smile on her face when she said that, and a twinkle in her eye, but Kerry knew that didn't mean she didn't believe what she was saying.

"The difference here is that we use violent magic only in self-defense, or in the defense of others. Y'all know Season well enough now to understand that there's no stoppin' her, short of killin' her. Now, there's plenty of witches out there who'd think we were evil to contemplate such a thing, but when it comes to evil, I have to think that letting Season continue her reign of terror is just about the worst thing a person could do."

"From what I've seen," Kerry said, "I'd have to agree."

"Of course." Mother Blessing spoke as if no other opinion was even worth considering. "Y'all have been touched by her foul deeds.

She's impacted your life. Those others, the ones who'd defend her, they don't know her like we do. They haven't lost two sons and a husband to her, or a lover, or a whole town full of neighbors and friends."

"That's probably true."

"Bet your sweet patootie it is," Mother Blessing said with a chuckle. "So the question is, what do we do about her? What steps are y'all willin' to take to make sure she can't keep doin' what she's been doin'?"

Kerry had thought long and hard about just that question. "Whatever it takes," she said decisively. "I'd do anything."

"I'm delighted to hear it, child." She wheeled in close to Kerry, leaning forward, her bulk almost spilling out of her scooter. "What's really required to go the extra step is depth of commitment. If you're willin' to go where the magic takes you, it'll carry the weight."

"I'm willing," Kerry affirmed. If she had any doubts along the way she could simply call up the pictures of Daniel and Josh emblazoned into her memory.

"That's fine, just fine." Mother Blessing wrapped her big, fleshy hands around Kerry's.

They felt warmer than human hands could rightfully be, as if they burned with the inner fire of her dark magics. Kerry would embrace that darkness, if it would lead to revenge. This was why she'd come here.

Then Mother Blessing released her hands and backed away from her, rolling toward a kitchen cupboard. She opened the door and withdrew a book—a slim volume, but covered in soft leather like Daniel's journals. It looked incredibly old, the leather creased and cracked, the pages yellow with age. Mother Blessing put it in her scooter's basket and drove close enough for Kerry to reach it. "Take the book, child," she said. "First thing you've got to do is learn the Old Tongue."

"What's that?" Kerry asked.

"The words of power. They come from a language forgotten by humans, a language that predates the written word. There was a time when magic was commonplace, swirling through the air like smog does today. People understood it better'n we do electricity today—'course, there wasn't as many people about, and not all of 'em knew how to use magic. But they all knew someone who did, and they respected their shamans, instead of burnin' 'em at the stake or forcin' 'em into hiding."

Kerry figured that there was some personal bias tinting Mother Blessing's commentary—if living a hermit's life in a disguised home deep in the Swamp wasn't being forced into hiding, she didn't know what was. Daniel, too, had been good at disguising his nature. And Season was nothing if not expert at running and hiding. If these three—the most powerful witches Kerry had ever imagined—were all forced into seclusion by the world's distrust of magic, then it was not surprising that Mother Blessing had strong feelings about the matter.

Taking the book from the basket, Kerry flipped through its brittle pages. At first glance, it was completely illegible. There were no words in it, not in any kind of writing she could decipher—just scribbles, seemingly random markings that might have been the scratchings of an animal's claws. She looked up, confused. "How am I supposed to . . . ?"

"Give it some time," Mother Blessing assured her. "Look it over at night, before you go to sleep."

Kerry closed the book and put it on the table, still confused but willing to give her the benefit of the doubt.

"When y'all speak the Old Tongue," Mother Blessing continued, "it draws the power of the Old Ones into you. Since y'all will be taught how to use that power, the right combination of words and gestures focuses the power and directs it where you want it. Gesture is as important as words, Kerry, and don't forget that. It's the combination that makes y'all's magic effective."

She pointed across the kitchen to where a copper-bottomed pot hung on the wall. "As a for instance," she said, "see that pot?"

"I see it."

"Okay, now watch me." Mother Blessing raised her hands and curled her fingers. She took her right hand and, with the thumb sticking up, tucked the two lower fingers flat against her palm, and crooked the middle two as if holding onto a pole. She splayed the fingers of her left hand as far apart as she could while bringing the thumb down crosswise across her palm. "Looks awkward, but it ain't bad," she explained. "You'll get used to it."

Pointing both hands toward the pot, she said a single word that sounded to Kerry like "bibblehead." As soon as the word had escaped her lips, the pot vibrated against the wall, shaking free of the hook that held it there, and floated across the room, as if carried by spectral hands, to land safely in the basket of Mother Blessing's scooter.

"What was that word?" Kerry asked her. Before she spoke it she made sure her own hands were neatly crossed on her lap, just in case. "'Bibblehead'?"

"B-I-B-E-L-H-E-T, I think," Mother Blessing spelled out. "Actual spellin' ain't all that important—it's the speakin' of it that counts. I couldn't define it, either, just know that it'll do what I want it to do. That's what y'all have got to achieve—the knowledge that the words and gestures'll be there when you need 'em, without having to think about 'em too much. Thinkin' things through'll get you killed. It's got to be automatic."

"But . . . that could take years!" Kerry complained. "You've been at it for what, centuries."

"That's right, child," Mother Blessing

agreed. "But once y'all start in to learning, you'll be surprised how fast it goes. Power feeds power, Kerry. It's like it's all floatin' out there lookin' for a home, like liquid searchin' for the lowest point, and when it finds one, it flows in fast and strong."

She took the pot from the basket and put it on the table in front of Kerry. "Put it back," she instructed.

Kerry started to rise, lifting the pot from the table. "No," Mother Blessing said sharply. "Not that way."

Kerry understood what she meant, but not how to accomplish the task. "But . . ."

"Do like this," Mother Blessing said. She folded the fingers of both hands toward her palms, making hooks of them, then raised the thumbs and pointed them toward the wall where the pot had been. She held her right hand about a hand's breadth higher than the left. Kerry duplicated the pose as best she could, until Mother Blessing nodded her satisfaction. "That's good," she said. "Now hold the pose."

Kerry did so, and Mother Blessing unfolded her own hands, lowering them to her handlebars. "Now, say the word '*beshitoon.*'"

"Beshi . . . ?"

"*Beshitoon,*" Mother Blessing repeated.

Kerry held the position with her hands and attempted the word. "Bes—*beshitoon,*" she said hesitantly.

Nothing happened.

"Say it like you mean it, child," Mother Blessing chided her.

Kerry hesitated a moment, her hands starting to quake from the effort of holding them still. She visualized the pot floating back across the room and hanging itself up on the hook again. *I can do this,* she thought. *Mother Blessing wouldn't be pushing me if she didn't know I could.*

"*Beshitoon.*"

The pot rattled on the tabletop, as if trying to make up its mind, then ascended into the air. Slowly, taking its time, but moving in almost precisely the line Kerry had visualized, it drifted across the room. Reaching the far wall, it lowered itself until the hook had slipped inside the hole in its handle. Then it was still, and the room silent.

"There you go," Mother Blessing said softly. "Nothin' to it, is there?"

I wouldn't say that, Kerry thought. But excitement coursed through her. She had *done* that! She had taken power from the air around her and directed it toward a specific goal, and that goal, however minor, had been achieved!

"I did magic," Kerry said finally. "I really did."

"You really did, child," Mother Blessing confirmed. "Congratulations."

Kerry Profitt's diary, November 4.

I did magic.

Yeah, I know, big whoop. I moved a pot. Could have used some scrubbing—the copper bottom was a bit on the tarnished side—but I didn't take it that far. One step at a time, right? Today I move, tomorrow I may scrub.

Or not.

The thing is, this is why I came to the Swamp. This is why I sought out Mother Blessing. She trained Daniel, right? So she can train me, too. Can, and more importantly, is willing to. Even anxious. She knows that Season is out of control. And the closer it gets to next year's Witches' Convocation, the more important it is to take Season out of commission.

Which means that I don't have much time to perfect my skills. I don't have centuries, or even years. I have weeks, months.

I was going to write in here last night, after my day's training, but instead I did as Mother Blessing suggested, and I looked through the book she gave me, the one with the Old Tongue in it. Look at it before you go to sleep, she had said, in that delightful accent of hers that makes everything sound like music. So I did. Still looked like chicken scratches to me.

But then I went to sleep, and in my dreams the writing became clear. It was so realistic that when I woke up, I grabbed the book and looked again. And guess what?

I could read it!

Well, not READ it, precisely. The words still don't make any sense, words like bibblehead and beshitoon. But it was as if they were all written down using our alphabet. No more scribbles and scratches. Don't ask me how—magic, I guess—but now at least I can sound out the words, know how I'm supposed to say them. I still need Mother Blessing to tell me which ones should be used for what, and what gestures to combine with them—seems like I'm particularly dangerous right now, because if I accidentally spoke one of them while unconsciously making some gesture or other, I could blow something up or hurt someone.

But yesterday I knew squat about this stuff, and today I've not only done magic, but I'm able to read the words in the book. Power flows to power, she says. The more I achieve, the more will come to me.

I wouldn't want to be Season Howe a couple of months from now. Because I intend to flow a lot of power this way, in a hurry.

Impatient, me? Perish the thought.

More later,

K.

17

Erin pounded on her door.

"You're going to miss class again, Beck!" she shouted. Rebecca tunneled deeper into her blankets, wedged a pillow over her head.

She didn't want to go to class. She didn't want to get out of bed. She hadn't wanted to since Halloween, since . . . since Josh had died at the hands of Season Howe.

She couldn't stop dwelling on the sight of Josh, murdered, body cooling up against a bank of slot machines. Every time she closed her eyes, it seemed, he was there—either that or the image of Season herself. She had become convinced now that she'd been right after all, at that séance—that Season was looking for them, hunting them down. If that was true, there was hardly any purpose in getting out of bed. When Season came for her, it wouldn't matter where she was.

Kerry, at least, was trying to learn how to defend herself against the witch. Rebecca didn't have that option. She was defenseless, and every day that she listened to Erin—every day that she got out of bed—she was only one day closer to the inevitable confrontation.

She knew that she was slipping into clinical depression. Erin had said as much, had even offered to take her down to the student health center and help her sign up for counseling. But Rebecca knew that no counseling could help her with her problem.

Every now and then she talked with Scott or Brandy—Kerry was out of reach again, and their little summer group was getting smaller and smaller—and that helped a little, mostly because she could speak freely with them, didn't have to hide what was really on her mind. But they were far away, and she was here in Santa Cruz, alone.

Erin knocked again and Rebecca shoved her pillow aside. "Okay!" she called. "I'm getting up, okay?"

"Fine," she heard Erin answer.

This would, she had decided, be the last

year she and Erin shared a place. She didn't know what would happen next year.

But then, she didn't know if she'd be alive by next year. Certainly not if Season Howe had anything to say about it.

There was, it turned out, a lot more to the whole witchcraft thing than simply reciting strange-sounding words and making funny hand motions. Mother Blessing made Kerry spend hours in the Swamp becoming intimately familiar with dwarf trillium, silky camellia, fiddlehead, and log fern, discerning Tupelo baldcypress from Atlantic white-cedar from maple-blackgum, tasting the bark of red maple, crushing pine needles in her hands and inhaling the bitter scent, picking bunches of paw paw, blackgum, devil's walking stick, and wild grapes for the table. Not all magic could simply be scooped from the ether, she explained. Some had to be distilled from plants and trees, teased from animals, dug from the very earth.

Kerry learned how to tell apart the tracks and scat of the swamp's big mammals: the paw of the bobcat and the black bear, the hoof of the white-tailed deer, the smaller track of gray fox and red, of raccoon and mink and gray squirrel. She came to recognize the calls of different warblers, the Swainson's and the Wayne's and the Myrtle, the chirps of the ovenbird and the hermit thrush, the sounds of the robins and blackbirds that swarmed in as the month progressed as if drawn by the fiery leaves on autumn trees. She took pleasure in the staccato rapping of the pileated woodpecker; she went to sleep at night wondering what the barred owl was talking about, or cringing at the plaintive cry of the bobcat; she woke to the *yakkety-yak* of the wood duck. With great care, Mother Blessing taught her to extract venom from the cottonmouth, the canebrake rattler, and the copperhead, and how to tell them apart from the dozen or so nonpoisonous varieties of snake that lived nearby.

Every night, Kerry went to bed with aching muscles and a head swimming with new information and vivid images, her tongue tripping over the foreign words and phrases she had learned that day. And each day she woke early and leapt from her bed, ready to repeat the process, to absorb more knowledge, to glean more wisdom from the Swamp and its inhabitants—and, of course, from Mother

Blessing herself. The days grew ever shorter—darkness came early now—but Kerry packed them full. Makeup was a thing of the past—a quick shower, a brush through her hair and a band to hold it back, some jeans and a sweater or maybe sweat pants and a long-sleeved T-shirt, and she was ready for the day. She barely took time to notice that her physical efforts were making her ever stronger, her arms and shoulders firm and supple, her waist tight, her thighs and calves bunched with strength.

When she was inside, she worked with Mother Blessing on learning the correct pronunciation of the Old Tongue, on practicing magical gestures until her hands screamed with aching. And she read, still working her way through Daniel's journals, front to back, beginning to end. She couldn't remember a time in her life that had been so filled with activity, days so long and with never a moment to be bored—hardly even any time, but for the few seconds between undressing and falling asleep, to reflect on anything.

During one of the rare moments of downtime, she had turned on the TV for the first time, and had not been at all surprised to find that it received more than a hundred channels, none of which seemed worth watching. This house was like that, though—she could take long, steaming showers without worrying that the hot water tank (if there was one; she had never seen it) would run out. The lights and the heat always worked, though there seemed to be no electrical or gas lines to the place. Mother Blessing could, she figured, solve the world's energy problems in seconds if she wanted to. But then the energy companies wouldn't be able to make any money, and they'd probably prove a far more nefarious adversary than even Season Howe.

Kerry knew that this was a time of preparation, a schooling time, but it didn't feel like a step on the way to somewhere; it felt like a destination achieved. As if she had already made it to where she was going.

It was, she decided one night in the moments before sound sleep overtook her, a happy time. In spite of everything that had led her to this point. She had rarely been quite so content.

She found that strange.

Now that I am older and have seen more of the wide world, I realize that there were great advantages to growing up where I did, to reaching maturity—and spending many months after that—in the Great Dismal. It was, and probably remains, a magical place to be a child, full of mystery and, yes, some danger. The sheer variety of plants and animals made every day an adventure: How many children my age went to school with alligators and came home with black bears? How many knew that every time they left the house there was the distinct possibility that, before suppertime, they could become hopelessly lost, never again to see their mother and brother? How many could see millions upon millions of blackbirds erupt from the Swamp, filling the sky in a steady stream that blacked out the sun for most of a day before they had all flown away?

Precious few, I'd wager. And though, in the way of small children everywhere, I didn't always appreciate it while it was happening, I certainly do now. I'm glad Mother Blessing didn't let Season drive her away from the Swamp, but only deep into it, that horrible day when she ruined Slocumb, house by house, burning each one with her magical fires until the screams of those inside faded away, keeping the flames hot until every trace of habitation was gone. Mother Blessing did the right thing by hiding out, by refusing to return to Slocumb until a safe period had passed, for in her fury Season Howe was certainly more than herself, channeling evil unknown and unknowable, not to be stopped by any earthly intercession.

But the Swamp: I was writing of the Swamp. Each day a new lesson, a new joy, sometimes a new fear, but always with Mother Blessing, and usually Abraham, to help me through it all. And so many surprises, for anyone willing to open his eyes and look for them. I met George Washington there, in 1763. I didn't know yet, of course, what a courageous leader of soldiers he would turn out to be, but he was already known as an intelligent man, and a decent one, with a sharp eye for business.

And one day in November of 1894 when I was back visiting Mother Blessing—depressed at my inability to find Season, who had been successfully avoiding me for months, and feeling like a complete disaster, a worthless fool who would never amount to anything—I met a sad-eyed young man roaming the Swamp on foot, looking, he said, for the best way to kill himself.

"Best," I asked, "in the sense of most assured? Or most dramatic?"

"I should like it to make a statement," he said after considering my question. "I believe I should like people to talk about it."

"Is there, perhaps, some certain individual who you would especially desire to hear the news?" I inquired, believing I was beginning to understand the nature of his predicament. He sat down on the log of a fallen gum tree and looked at me as if deciding whether or not I was trustworthy enough to reveal his story to.

"I was late in Canton, Massachusetts," said he at length, "where I surprised my lady love by arriving unannounced at her door bearing a most special gift. I thought that this lady would welcome me. Certainly I hoped so, having ridden all night by train."

"What was the gift?" I asked the young man.

"Two books of poetry, written especially with her in mind," he said. "One for her and the other for me. There existed only the one copy of each book. But upon being given hers, she simply held it at arm's length, as though I had given her a toad or a snake, and closed the door on me.

"In my grief, I wandered back to the railroad yard and tore my own volume to shreds. On the journey home, I determined that without Miss White, I had no reason to live. So I am here, in the most aptly named Great Dismal, where I should like to find an appropriately dramatic way to close the door on my existence."

I scratched my chin again and considered his predicament. "Hmmm," I said. "A number of options present themselves. Have you considered trying to make the acquaintance of a brown bear, or an alligator, or perhaps a poisonous snake? Although any of those might leave you merely crippled or ill, not dead. Perhaps you could find a tree in the process of being felled and stand on the wrong side of it; the woodcutters, though, might see you and insist you move away."

"You seem quite well versed in the ways the Swamp can put finish to a fellow."

"Swamp born and bred, sir, though I have traveled more than a little in my day."

He regarded me for a long time, nodding his head. Finally he said, "I suppose the most certain way would be to walk into the swamp with no provisions. One way or another I should not survive the journey."

"That seems to work, yes," I agreed.

"But if my body was never found, then the news of my passing might never reach Miss White."

"It is true," I said, "that she would likely never know with certainty."

The young man raised his arms in evident frustration. "What is the point of it?" he thundered. "To come all this way, to the most dismal spot in Creation, and still not find a suitable end?"

"Very little point that I can see," I agreed again.

The young man spared me a smile

then, the first that I had seen, and it was like a flicker of sunshine breaking through storm clouds. "Then perhaps it is my plan that is faulty, and the better course would be to go on living after all."

I pointed my index finger at him. "And to live such a life that Miss White would learn to regret having spurned you," I added.

He smiled again, this time as if the sun had warmed the sky and burned the clouds away. "Yes," he said happily. "I think that might be the better course of action after all."

"I am happy to hear it," I told the man.

He took my hand then, and shook it with great effusiveness. "I thank you, sir. Be well, and remember the name of Robert Frost, in the event that some day it should come to mean something to anyone. Especially to Miss Elinor White."

I gave him my own name, and he smiled again and walked away. I felt better about myself immediately: Having saved a life, I felt the depression that had *gripped me lift at once, and I knew that I would, in fact, find Season again and destroy her.*

And that young man? He did become something special after all.

I remember the story today because I heard on the radio that Robert Frost died yesterday. While I don't believe he was a witch or prolonged his life through any special magical powers, there was certainly magic within that man. He won four Pulitzer prizes for his magnificent poetry, and just over two years ago he became the first poet to read a poem at the inauguration of an American president.

I, for one, salute his passing—much delayed, and we are all the better for that. And his moving on serves to remind me of the special joys and pleasures of life in the Great Dismal, so thank you, Mr. Frost, for all your gifts.

I remain,
Daniel Blessing, January 30, 1963

18

Just when Kerry was starting to think that her life was destined to be devoted to studying and nothing else, Mother Blessing surprised her.

"How long's it been since you got yourself a new outfit, honey?" she asked one morning, startling Kerry from her reading. She was constantly amazed by the things Daniel had seen and done, by the sweep of history he had lived. But the idea that he had effectively saved the life of Robert Frost, whose poetry she had loved in high school, had blown her away. She had been reflecting on that when Mother Blessing mentioned her wardrobe, and the disconnect seemed almost surreal. "I swear, the clothes you're wearin' look like they're fixin' to come apart at the seams."

Honestly, Kerry hadn't even been thinking about clothes, or hair or makeup or anything else. There didn't seem to be time in the day for such things, and there was no one to get dressed up for except Mother Blessing. Since the older woman's idea of dolling herself up usually involved wearing stretch pants with slightly fewer stains than usual, Kerry felt that the bar of presentability had been lowered, and that was fine with her. Now that Mother Blessing mentioned it, though, Kerry remembered that there was a certain therapeutic value to shopping that she appreciated.

"I guess it's been a while," she answered. She didn't want to sound too anxious, though, in case this was some kind of test. "If you think we have time . . ."

Mother Blessing's smile looked genuine, though. She was not an attractive woman, but when she really smiled, a sense of true joy showed through. "Child, we don't answer to nobody but ourselves. We want to make the time, then that's just what we'll do."

A simulacrum rowed Kerry and Mother Blessing out of the swamp in the old witch's boat, to where the creek went right up behind Edgar Brandvold's property in Wallaceton, Virginia. Edgar was a man who looked as old as Mother Blessing was, though he couldn't have been more than eighty or so, whereas Mother Blessing, while she looked like someone in her fifties, was obviously several hundred years old. When they arrived, the simulacrum lifted Mother Blessing's scooter up onto old Edgar's driveway, then lifted her up onto it. She cruised up to the front door of Edgar's sagging frame house, which looked as much like a shack as the magical facade of Mother Blessing's place, and rapped on his door. A few minutes later a stoop-shouldered mass of wrinkles with thick glasses and a knob-headed cane came out, waved, smiled at Kerry and the simulacrum as if he'd known them both for decades, and unlocked his garage, a former carriage house that looked to be in even worse shape than the main house.

"Howdy, Mother Blessin'!" he called loudly. His voice was deep and sonorous, unexpected in such an apparently ancient fellow. He wore baggy brown pants and a plaid shirt under a ratty blue cardigan sweater, like some kind of Mr. Rogers gone to seed. "Lovely day. You gon' take a ride?"

"That's right, Edgar," Mother Blessing answered brightly. "Miss Kerry here's got some shoppin' she needs to get done."

Edgar opened the carriage house doors widely and Kerry saw her van in its shadowed interior. "What's that doing here?" she asked. Last time she had seen it, it was still parked in its spot near the old Slocumb site, on the other side of the Great Dismal.

"I had it brought around," Mother Blessing explained. "Thought it'd be best if Edgar kept an eye on it."

The simulacrum stepped toward Edgar, who seemed well accustomed to such temporary creatures, and took the key from the old man's hand. "Y'all drive safe now, hear?" Edgar said.

"Always do," Mother Blessing answered for the voiceless being, which opened the driver's door and climbed up behind the wheel.

"I could drive," Kerry offered, a little fearful about the reactions other motorists might have to the plainly nonhuman thing.

"Wouldn't hear of it," Mother Blessing

replied, shaking her hands at the very idea. "Ain't nothing like havin' a chauffeur take you where you need to go."

"But he's . . . not exactly convincing," Kerry argued.

"Folks see what they expect to see," Mother Blessing insisted. "Or if I'm around, what I want 'em to see."

The simulacrum at least seemed to know what it was doing. It backed the van smoothly out of the long, narrow garage, then stopped and climbed out, leaving the engine idling. Opening the big side door, it easily lifted Mother Blessing off her scooter, as if she were weightless, and deposited her in the front passenger seat. Then it put the scooter up into the cargo area of the van. There was a single back seat with a seat belt, and at Mother Blessing's suggestion Kerry got into that. The van had a distinctly earthy aroma to it, but she didn't know if that was from sitting cooped up in a small garage by a creek, or from the presence of the simulacrum, who was composed of leaves, vines, mud, and other swamp debris, in the enclosed space. The simulacrum got back behind the wheel and put the van in gear. With a cheery farewell to old Edgar, they headed up the road toward Norfolk.

"One thing I've been wondering about," Kerry began, after they'd been driving a few minutes. Seeing Edgar Brandvold looking so much older than Mother Blessing had reminded her of her curiosity. "If it's not too personal to ask."

"Well, y'all just ask it, and if it's too personal I won't be shy about sayin' so," Mother Blessing replied.

"It's just . . . Daniel looked like he was in his late twenties or early thirties. Season looks like mid-thirties at the oldest. You look like someone in her fifties, maybe. But I know you're all much older than that—so how exactly does the aging process work for witches? Now that I'm learning, will I stop aging and always look like this?"

Mother Blessing regarded her for a few moments, as if she were weighing the relative merits of appearing to be a teenager for hundreds of years. "It's mostly a function of peak power," she said then. "It takes different witches different lengths of time to achieve their strongest capabilities. At that time, the aging process more or less freezes up. I guess I was a slow learner, and it wasn't until I was in my fifties that I reached my peak. My overall health was better—that's gone downhill in recent years, I'm afraid, though I'm still not aging much."

Kerry nodded. "That makes sense, I guess."

"Don't much matter if it does or not," Mother Blessing answered. "It's how it is."

Twenty minutes later, they turned into the parking lot of a huge, shining Wal-Mart. "They'll have everything y'all might need here," Mother Blessing announced.

Kerry couldn't prevent the crestfallen expression from washing over her face. She still had plenty of money left over from her college account; since reaching the Swamp, the only thing she'd had to spend it on was the brief trip to Las Vegas. "Isn't there a mall someplace?"

Mother Blessing eyed her with surprise for a moment, then smiled. "Turn around," she told the driver, who obeyed instantly—had, in fact, been starting to obey before the witch gave the verbal command. "'Course there's a mall. Teenage girl needs more than a place like this, don't she? Let's us find you somewhere with real shops."

In the dream, I'm driving in a car. This one I can remember, so I don't think it's the same dream I used to have in the weeks before I met Daniel. Nothing special about the car—it's not the van I bought or any particular car at all that I can tell. But I'm stuck in traffic.

And as I'm sitting there, looking at all the other cars around me, wishing I could just floor it and move already, water starts to bubble up through the floorboards. (Were they ever actual boards, at one time? Just a digression. They sure aren't now.)

Rapidly, the water rises. I try to open a door or a window to let it out, but nothing doing. I can't get anything open. Now I'm in water up to my waist—it's not cold, I notice, but pleasantly body temperature, and I'm not nearly as panicked as I probably should be. Still, it rises.

And rises. And then it's over my head, and I'm still there, seatbelted in, unable to go anywhere or do anything about it. Noises sound funny, like, you know, when you're underwater. Finally, I notice, traffic eases up a little and I can move again. I press the accelerator down and start to edge forward, unable to breathe now, my lungs constricting, really and truly beginning to drown.

But as I do, I'm looking out the car windows at the other cars around and I see that the drivers of those are all underwater inside their cars too. Only the thing is, they don't seem to mind. They're breathing normally—well, normally if humans could breathe underwater. Bubbles float up from their mouths and noses, but they look just like people do in traffic, some smiling, some talking, some angry or impatient. Just people in cars. And we're all underwater.

But I'm the only one who's drowning.

Once again, I need Doc Brandy to tell me just what this all means, and she's not around. Brandy ain't handy.

My guess? Maybe it's telling me that I'm becoming different from all the normal people out there, the people who are not witches—or even halfway to becoming one. Alienation from my peers. Evidence of my journey and how it diverts from that of everyone else I've ever known.

Or not. Who knows?

More later,

K.

"Strike!"

Kerry heard Mother Blessing's voice in her head, even though the woman was miles away, back in her cabin. She had drilled Kerry on this so many times, though, it seemed as if she were right here with her. Kerry did as she'd been taught: She hurled herself to the peat, tucking her head, rolling on one shoulder, and coming up on her feet, hands splayed out in the proper ritualistic position. "*Hastamel!*" she shouted as she rose, and a burst of energy shot from her hands, tearing a chunk of vegetation off the simulacrum with which she sparred. The thing grunted with pain—part of Mother Blessing's commitment to realism, Kerry figured—and dropped to its knees. Kerry knew she'd missed any vital organs, so she repositioned her hands and spoke a defensive spell. If the thing had been a witch, it could have gotten off a blast.

Since it wasn't, she only defended herself against an imaginary spell, and then she shot an impulse wave at it. The creature's head separated from its shoulders and it went down hard in the dirt. Kerry allowed herself a congratulatory moment, but she cut it short when a noise behind her alerted her to the fact that this one hadn't been alone.

She spun around, throwing up a blocking spell and then following that with another sharp, directed burst that punched a hole the size of a soccer ball through this one's chest. These sparring matches were wearying, and she became frustrated when there was one opponent after another after another, even sometimes half a dozen all at once. But they were also necessary, she knew. Daniel had found himself in all kinds of dangerous situations over the course of his long life, and—until that last battle—had survived them all. If Kerry was going to survive, she needed to train until she dropped, and then pick herself up and train some more.

She may have resented Mother Blessing while she was putting herself through the mental and physical agony of the exercise, but when it saved her life some day, she'd thank her mentor. She tried to keep sight of that knowledge, to let it help her through these difficult days.

The second simulacrum fell, and Kerry found that there were only two, for now. She was allowed a moment's respite, a chance to catch her breath and let her racing heart calm a bit. After a few minutes the swamp's normal sounds resumed: Birds cried, insects buzzed, a faraway frog croaked its basso profundo solo.

Kerry stood for a few moments, just enjoying the day. It was cold enough in the swamp that she had the hood of her new lime-green fleece snugged around her head, and fake fur–lined boots with a fake suede finish— bought out of consideration for Josh's feelings about wearing real leather—on her feet, but the sky was crisp and cloudless. Between the flame-red tops of two maples she watched a great blue heron skate across the sky and out of sight. Her appreciation for the natural world was far greater than it had ever been now that she had a better sense of how inextricably humanity was tied to it.

I wish Rebecca were here, she thought, *and Brandy and Scott, too. I wish they could all go through what I have, learn what I have.* She'd had other friends, of course. But with the loss of her parents, and then her ordeal over the summer, most of those people had drifted away from her. She didn't miss anyone from

Northwestern, not really. She barely thought of them at all, except a couple of times when she found herself imagining how much Dr. Manning, her history professor, would love to talk to Mother Blessing and hear some early American history from someone who'd been there. But Rebecca, Scott, and Brandy—they held important positions in her heart, and she couldn't help believing each would find valuable lessons here in the Swamp, even if they didn't care to learn magic.

It's not magic to understand that what happens to nature affects all of us, she thought. *To know that the wholesale extinction of species can only be bad for everyone, that humans won't be the last species to become extinct, or that no species except humans has ever been single-handedly responsible for the extinction of any other. And it doesn't take magic to comprehend that power flows from nature through us, or that we have to give back to nature some of what we take from it, if we want the interrelationship to continue.*

Kerry laughed. *Listen to me,* she thought, even though she hadn't spoken a word out loud, not wanting to disturb the Swamp's natural choir with a human voice. *I sound like some kind of green. And I thought Rebecca was our resident hippie.* But she wasn't thinking along political lines, or about social policy, just about what Mother Blessing had taught her of the need to respect nature and worship it as a manifestation of the Old Ones from whom all witchy power sprang. Along with that respect, which also applied to her tools—her cauldron, her athame, her wand, and the rest of the things Mother Blessing had helped her make or find—came a new appreciation. No tree, rock, implement, or person lasted forever. While it was in one's life, then, it had to be cared for and held precious.

The faintest rustle of a footfall on dry leaves alerted her, and Kerry spun, dropping to a crouch and raising her hands in a warding gesture. *"Shellitush!"* she shouted, generating a protective field around her. But this wasn't a simulacrum, she saw. Instead, emerging from the cover of a nearby cypress stump, an enormous black bear regarded her, one paw up on the stump, one hanging free, back feet firmly on the ground. Its head bobbed a little, as if listening to some silent tune, but its nose wrinkled slightly and she suspected it was sniffing her, catching the odor that sailed on a barely perceptible breeze. Its eyes were obsidian; its mouth open, tongue lolling over big teeth in an accidental impression of a smile. The big animal looked happy, even friendly. But she knew that it was not. Not that it would intentionally hurt her. If it felt threatened or trapped, it would certainly try. Otherwise, it bore her no ill will, just as surely as it didn't want to be her friend.

Kerry tried to project her thoughts toward the bear. She wasn't a meal, she wasn't a danger. She was simply a mildly interesting side note in the day's activities. After a few moments, as if it understood, the bear dropped down from the trunk, turned around, and loped away into the brush.

Kerry glanced toward the simulacra, both of which had decomposed back into the swamp stuff from which they were made, and then disappeared. She had a long walk back to the cabin, and the day was getting no warmer. Looking for the position of the sun to catch her bearings, Kerry headed for home.

19

"I died once," Scott said. "You didn't know that, huh?"

Brandy looked across the table at him. Mugs of hot chocolate steamed between them, and outside bundled-up students rushed to and fro, slipping on icy sidewalks. It would get colder, but already the weather had turned sour. Thanksgiving was tomorrow, and Scott wanted an invitation to her place for the day—an invitation that would not be offered.

She and Scott had agreed to get together twice a week for lunch, coffee, or sometimes dinner or a movie. Not dating—she wouldn't go that far, and at her insistence it was strictly hands off. When they'd returned from Las Vegas, she had declared that it was over between them. He had packed up his things and moved out, leaving her in an apartment that she had to struggle to pay for. She had considered getting a roommate, but there was only one bedroom, and she valued her privacy. So far, her parents were helping out, but she knew she would have to move after the first of the year.

"No," she answered. She took a sip of the hot chocolate. It had been topped with whipped cream and just a hint of cinnamon. "No, I don't think I did. You never told me, did you?"

"No, it's . . . it's weird," he said. "I don't talk about it, really. I thought about it, after . . . you know, after Mace died. And then in Vegas, with Josh and everything. But it didn't seem appropriate, somehow. Because I came back, and they didn't."

"You came back? I mean, obviously, you're here. But what happened?" It seemed like the kind of thing a guy would tell someone he was in love with, living with. But hearing it this way just helped cement her conclusion that Scott wasn't ready for a real commitment.

He looked away from her when he told the story. These meetings were hard on him,

Brandy knew, but still he insisted he wanted them. She was convinced that he thought she would reconsider, take him back.

He was wrong.

"I was eight," he said. "My dad was driving, mom in the front seat, me in back. I was wearing my seat belt, of course, but I was kind of laying down in the seat, you know, flopping around like kids do. We were going through an intersection when some maniac in a big pickup truck ran a red light and slammed right into us. Dad says the car spun around a dozen times, but he's always been kind of prone to exaggeration. Anyway, we bounced off a couple of other cars, slammed into a light pole. The car was almost cut in half, and I was banged up pretty bad. The paramedics on the scene thought I was gone—they actually wrote me off and went to work on my mom, who was the one with the most minor injuries. There happened to be a doctor there, and he didn't have any trauma equipment or anything, but he checked my pulse, my breathing. He declared me dead.

"I don't remember any of this—I only remember being told about it later on, when I was older. But after they had all turned their backs on me, I revived somehow. I started to scream, and they were really freaked out that I was even alive."

"I can see how that might be surprising," Brandy admitted.

"Yeah. I was out for a couple minutes, I guess. My mom said if it had been any longer they would have worried about long-term brain damage. She said she'd never been so glad to hear me holler bloody murder."

"I bet." Scott's mom was a little stiff, a little too old–New England for her tastes, but still a nice enough lady.

Scott drank some cocoa, went quiet for a minute. Finally, he put his mug down, ran a finger across his lips to wipe away any chocolate remnants. "So anyway," he said, "I guess the moral of the story is that you don't always know for sure if something is really dead. Sometimes it'll surprise you."

And there it is, Brandy thought. *He doesn't give up easily. You almost have to admire that.*

Almost.

She wasn't about to get sucked into it, though. She made up an excuse and left him in

the coffee shop. Ten minutes later she was sliding down the sidewalks herself. It *was* over. It
was because she said it was, and one person
didn't make a couple all by himself, no matter
how much he wanted it.

Anyway, she thought, *he only wants it because
Kerry's not here.*

They hadn't heard from her since leaving
Vegas. She had gone back to the swamp, back
to finish her training, she had said. After Josh's
death, none of them had had much to say to
one another. Kerry, Rebecca, and Scott had all
retreated into their own minds, into their own
worlds. She had done the same, Brandy knew.
They had promised to stay in touch, and
Rebecca had called a couple of times since
then, and of course she still saw Scott.

But everything had changed. Brandy had
realized it was changing even before Josh's
death, but that had hurried it along, made it all
somehow more definitive.

Life might be short. *Too short to waste in a
relationship in which you're only a stand-in for
someone else,* she decided. She didn't know if
Season was really hunting them, although it
certainly seemed as if that might be the case.

If she was, then Brandy had a lot of living to squeeze into a finite amount of time. Being with Scott wasn't really how she wanted to spend it.

So she had moved on. She just hoped he would be able to do the same.

Thanksgiving brought a perfect fall day, with a clear sky, a snap to the air, and leaves like brittle flame. Kerry rowed herself to the Slocumb site and tugged the skiff up onto the bank at the edge of that blasted, forsaken landscape. She had listened to some of Mother Blessing's stories about that fateful day, and had read various accounts of it in Daniel's journals. It had made such an impression on his mother, and through her on his own life, that he came back to it again and again.

Kerry found herself drawn to the place too, trying to picture what it had been like on that day so long ago. She walked across the scorched earth, noting the location of each building. Season had burned each one individually to the ground. The places where the roads had been laid out were still clearly distinguishable, now that she knew what to look for, and where structures had been, fire-blackened earth made precise geometric shapes. Wind had blown across this land, softening the edges, but as she'd noticed before, not a blade of grass had grown here since that time, not a dandelion or one of the ferns that were everywhere just a few feet away.

She had never quite understood how Mother Blessing had such precise knowledge of Season's actions on that day, since by her own account she had taken refuge in the swamp as soon as it became clear that Season's rage had made her too powerful to fight. Kerry had asked, a time or two, but Mother Blessing had glossed over the issue as skillfully as a math teacher dodging the question of just when in life someone might have a need for advanced trigonometry. Probably, she had just relived the incident so many times in her own mind that she thought she remembered things she couldn't possibly have seen. At any rate, the damage had been done, that long-ago day. The Swamp had grown back, even after the fire that burned for months afterward—everyplace but here, of course. Mother Blessing had lived, had borne her sons and raised them. The world kept turning.

But for the people of Slocumb, the people Mother Blessing had known, had lived among, the world had ended that day. Kerry didn't know if Season's murderous ways had begun that day—if, having snapped, she'd never fully regained her sanity—or if she'd already embraced evil, and in fact had been responsible for the initial killings that had led up to the day's events

Really, Kerry thought, *it doesn't matter. Season can't keep killing people I care about. Or strangers, for that matter. She's got to be stopped.*

She still had a lot to learn, a lot of drilling, a lot of practice before magic became as second nature to her as it would need to be to take on Season. But she was already more powerful than she had been three weeks ago when Josh had been killed, and a far more imposing person than she was a few months ago when she was trying to be a student at Northwestern, wanting nothing more than an "ordinary" life.

There is, she decided, *very little value to being ordinary.*

But there were times she wished for life to be a bit more like what she had grown up expecting, and this was one of them. The days and weeks had flown by; Thanksgiving was upon them. As a little girl, she had always loved that day, enjoying the televised parades, the football games, the way the house smelled, the warmth of her mother's kitchen, and the good spirits of the friends and relatives who came over. Mother Blessing's house couldn't be the same, but being there, so close to the region where the first European settlers made their homes, Kerry felt that some celebration was warranted. The older witch had agreed, so Kerry had gone out to shop for the requisite groceries: a turkey that Mother Blessing would fry, Southern style, in a deep pot she owned, and stuffing, cranberry sauce, fresh potatoes, green beans, and whatever else crossed her mind when she got to the market.

After spending a few minutes at the Slocumb site, soaking in the atmosphere and seeing it differently now that she had heard more stories about it, she rowed all the way over to Edgar Brandvold's place. He came out and unlocked the carriage house for her, wishing her a very happy Thanksgiving and revealing that he planned to spend the afternoon watching football. Kerry got in the minivan and drove to Deep Creek, where the nearest grocery store was. She loaded up with the things she needed and a few incidentals—Nehi and Coca-Cola for Mother Blessing, some herbal teas and a couple of bags of chocolate for herself—and took it all back to the van.

She appreciated Edgar Brandvold's willingness to garage the van for her. She had always been worried that someone would happen across it when she left it out in the open near Slocumb, and though it hadn't happened yet, hunting season had started and the Swamp was full of strangers. Now that she had met Edgar and knew he was an ally of Mother Blessing's, she felt comfortable asking him to help out.

When she pulled into his long drive, though, she knew at once that something was wrong. Edgar was nowhere to be seen, even when she honked her horn, and the door to his ramshackle house hung open. She remembered that when he'd come out before, it had been closed, and that he had closed it behind him with the unstudied efficiency of long habit. He didn't seem like the kind of man who'd forget and leave it open.

She killed her engine and climbed out of the van. The house and yard were quiet; only the ticking of her van and the cry of some far-away bird broke the silence. Dust that she had kicked up driving in hung on the still air.

Edgar's house was old, and the boards that composed it looked as if they'd never been painted, though surely they had been once. A gallery edged the front and one side, and the roof bowed low over the door. Missing shingles gave it a gap-toothed look. The house's windows were black, empty. Through the open front door Kerry could see nothing at all.

Steeling herself, fear welling up inside her, she walked across the yard and put her right foot on the first of three steps up to the gallery. The wood beneath her was worn thin, with nails sticking up from it. Old Edgar wasn't big on maintenance, that much was clear. Kerry had already announced her presence by honking, so she climbed the stairs and rapped her knuckles against the open door.

"Mr. Brandvold!" she called. Now she could see an entryway with a small side table for keys or mail and a worn staircase beyond. Her words echoed in the small space but were not answered.

She went in. "Mr. Brandvold, are you here?" The loud creak of a floorboard underfoot startled her, cranking up her anxiety another notch. In spite of the cool day she felt sweat beading on her lip. She went through a doorway into a parlor jammed with enough furniture for a whole house: chairs, sofas, a TV, a table holding a radio and several magazines, other tables in front of the chairs and sofas and lining the walls behind them, and lamps, all turned off, scattered here and there through it all.

Edgar Brandvold sat in one of the chairs, hands at his sides, eyes open. He looked relaxed, like a man peacefully watching television. But his blue cardigan sweater was purpled and moist, and fat, lazy flies were walking around on it.

His knob-headed cane had been driven through his heart.

Kerry caught the coppery smell of blood—and something else at the same time. The second smell was familiar, but it took her a moment to place it. A smell that reminded her of electricity.

Then it came to her.

The stink of ozone. The smell of destructive magic, of murder.

She turned and ran from the house, dashed across the yard, threw herself into the van and slammed her fist down on the door lock. She hadn't taken the key out of the ignition, so she cranked it, and as the engine roared to life she stomped down on the accelerator, cutting a wide arc across the yard as she sped away.

It wasn't until she was back on the road toward Deep Creek that she realized her mistake. This had been no ordinary killing. This could only be the work of Season Howe. She must have tortured Edgar to learn the whereabouts of Mother Blessing—which meant that Kerry needed to get into the Swamp, back to Mother Blessing, as fast as she could. Instead of driving away, she should have thrown the skiff into the creek and rowed for her life. Convincing herself to go back to Edgar's place, though, was almost beyond her capability, even though the only other place she knew her way well enough from was the Slocumb site . . . and if there was one place she didn't want to go while Season was around, that was it.

Choices . . .

The highway was empty, so when she jammed her foot down on the brake there was no one behind her to smash into her van's rear. She performed a shaky three-point turn and headed back the way she had come, back toward Wallaceton.

Back toward Season's last known location.

Chances were, though, that Season had already moved on. Obviously, she had determined that Edgar was connected in some way with Mother Blessing. So if he knew enough to tell her, before his horrible end, how to find Mother Blessing, then Season was already in the Swamp, and there was precious little time for Kerry to warn her mentor. If he did not, though, then Season would be looking for some other clue, and chances were, Slocumb would be on her list of destinations.

Kerry raced back into Edgar's yard, pulled as close to the creek as she dared, and dragged her skiff out of the van. She spared a moment's thought for the groceries and then abandoned them. There would be no Thanksgiving anyway, if Season got to Mother Blessing before she did. Climbing into the boat, she sat down and dipped her paddle in the water, glad that the autumn's activities had built her muscles. She would need to row as she never had before.

20

By the time Kerry reached Mother Blessing's home—*my home,* she thought defiantly, *as much as anyplace else is*—the once-blue sky had turned dark gray and begun to weep. She grounded the skiff at the edge of the small property and ran inside.

"Mother Blessing!" she called anxiously. "Are you—"

The door to Mother Blessing's bedroom banged open and the old witch rolled out into the hallway on her familiar scooter. Her brow was furrowed, her lips tightly compressed. "I know, child," she said. "Season is in the Swamp."

"Edgar . . ." Kerry began, barely able to formulate a sentence. "She killed him!"

"I thought as much," Mother Blessing

acknowledged. "I have eyes in the Swamp, Kerry. I know she's lookin' for us. Lookin' for me. It's not too late for y'all to get yourself gone, though. Things are like to turn ugly round here."

Kerry hadn't considered running for a moment, couldn't quite believe Mother Blessing was making the offer. "It's my fight too."

Mother Blessing spared her a smile at that. "I was hopin' you'd feel that way. Let's get to work."

"How do you get ready for something like this?" Kerry asked anxiously. She could hear the first heavy drops of a hard rain hammering against the roof. "When Daniel was preparing to battle Season, he locked himself in a room and I heard the strangest noises—bells, wind, screams."

Mother Blessing rolled toward the kitchen as she answered. "He took himself out of the world for a few minutes, sounds like," she said. "Purifyin' is important before a fight, if there's time. If he was pressed for time, then he'd have done it by goin' someplace where time has a different meaning, where a short spell for you was a day or more for him."

"You mean . . . when I was standing out-side the room waiting for him, he wasn't even in there?"

The old witch opened the refrigerator and rummaged around inside. "Yes and no," she said. "There's no easy answer to a question like that, and no right one either."

Kerry was almost afraid to ask the next one. "Are we . . . going someplace like that?"

"We don't even have that much time," Mother Blessing answered quickly. "We just got to be as pure as we are."

Kerry thought about making a crack to the effect that the only man she'd spoken with in a month was in his eighties and dead, but it didn't seem funny, even to her. She let it go and watched Mother Blessing's prepara-tions. As a sudden fierce wind began howling outside, her mentor took out potions made long ago and stored in glass bottles in the ice-box, then wheeled around and retrieved vari-ous implements from her cupboards. These were, for the most part, things Kerry hadn't seen before: a long sword she was sure she'd need both hands to lift, an old thorned stick that could be used as a wand, and, most frighteningly, a rifle or shotgun, Kerry wasn't sure which.

"What's that for?" Kerry asked, surprised. "Daniel didn't use anything like that."

"And he lost, didn't he?" Mother Blessing answered, her words clipped, her voice glacial. "I don't intend to."

Kerry couldn't argue with that, so she held her tongue. Mother Blessing moved rapidly, mixing the contents of some of the bottles, lighting candles, chanting softly to herself in words that Kerry recognized as the Old Tongue, even though she couldn't make out the meaning. Once Mother Blessing had combined some of the various fluids, she rubbed the mixture on the blade of the sword. She poured another concoction into a bowl, where it steamed like something from a mad-scientist movie, and into that she emptied a box of bullets. Her efficiency was wondrous to behold, even as her actions filled Kerry's heart with terror.

Mother Blessing pointed at the bowl of ammunition and tossed Kerry a dishtowel. "Dry those," she instructed. Kerry held her hand over the rim of the bowl and poured the liquid out into the sink, cringing inwardly as the cold steel of the bullets bumped against her flesh. She spread the towel on the counter and scooped them out onto it, then folded it over them and rubbed them dry. She had always hated guns; the thought that she might be asked to use one repulsed her. After a moment she checked the bullets.

"They're dry."

"Load it," Mother Blessing said.

Kerry looked at the forbidding weapon. "I . . . I don't know how."

Mother Blessing huffed at her and took the gun in her own hands, drawing the towel toward herself over the counter. Kerry felt like she ought to apologize, but then thought better of it. The woman had no reason to assume that Kerry would know how to use a rifle; she shouldn't get upset when it turned out she didn't.

Still, it was true that while Mother Blessing did almost all of the preparatory work, Season—if the weather outside was any indicator, and Kerry couldn't help feeling like it must be—was drawing ever closer. The rain beat at the roof and walls like fists, causing her to wonder if it had turned to hail. The wind buffeted the walls, seeping in through whatever cracks it could. In fifteen minutes the temperature had dropped at least thirty degrees.

Before Kerry could even process the drastic meteorological changes, though, there was a noise like a clap of thunder right outside. The whole house shook as if a sixteen-wheeler had run into it. Mother Blessing looked up at Kerry with a wry grin. "She's here."

"Do we have any simulacra?" Kerry asked.

"If she's outside, she's already gone through them."

"But . . . are we ready?" Kerry asked.

The witch was already in motion, wheeling her scooter around and heading out of the kitchen, toward the front door. "As we're gonna be. Got no time to be readier." Over her shoulder, she added, "Bring that stuff, willya?"

Kerry gathered up the sword, the stick, and the loaded gun and followed her. She caught up to Mother Blessing just inside the front door, where, to her astonishment, the older woman was climbing off the scooter. She had never seen Mother Blessing stand or walk, and had just assumed that both were impossible for her. But she was doing both now, and though her bulk made it difficult, she was able to maneuver herself to some degree. She tugged open the door, which blew inward with a great gust of wind, and stepped out into the lashing rain.

"This is still the South," Mother Blessing declared loudly. Kerry couldn't see who the witch was talking to, but she knew just the same. "We're hospitable folks here—y'all don't need to raise such a ruckus just to visit."

As Mother Blessing took a couple more steps away from the door, Kerry came closer to it and was able to see Season Howe standing on the firm ground outside the house. She couldn't spot any indication of how Season had arrived—there was no boat visible, nor any other form of transportation. But then again, Kerry couldn't see much; the curtain of rain reduced visibility to just a few yards.

Season looked like she had the last time Kerry had seen her: stern, severe, but undeniably beautiful. Her honey-blond hair was plastered to her head by the rain; wet black leathers, like a motorcyclist's, hugged her slim figure. Arms folded over her chest, she stared up at Mother Blessing on the wooden walkway outside the house, spared a casual glance for Kerry, whose arms were still laden with Mother Blessing's weapons, then looked back at the real threat.

"I decided I'm tired of you sending intermediaries after me," Season said, her voice calm and even. "Especially after I saw in Las Vegas that you are using these children again." Here her gaze ticked toward Kerry for a moment. "And not even children versed in the craft, but simply cannon fodder. You should be ashamed."

"Not that y'all will believe me," Mother Blessing argued, "but those 'children' weren't workin' on my behalf. They got their own issues with you."

"Is that right? I thought *you* were the one who wanted my hide—you and the sons you sacrificed."

Kerry was close enough to Mother Blessing to feel her go tense at that—*surprising,* she thought, *because I've been tense for a couple of hours now*—the woman's spine straightening, her fists clenching. "You leave them out of this."

"If you had left them out of it, they'd still be alive," Season observed. There was no cruelty in her tone, though there obviously was in the words she spoke. Mother Blessing took another step toward her.

"This house is under protection," she warned.

"And how far does that extend?" Season asked, almost cheerfully. "Since you're outside the house."

"Far enough."

The two witches faced each other, neither speaking for a moment. Kerry couldn't see Mother Blessing's eyes, but she was sure they were locked on Season's. The very air between them seemed charged somehow, as if to step into their path would be inviting electrocution.

"This has gone on too long," Season said after a few moments. Her voice sounded tighter now, as if she were starting to feel the tension. "Let's end it."

"Sounds good to me," Mother Blessing agreed. She raised her hands in a gesture with which Kerry had grown very familiar. *Lahatsi,* she thought, even before her mentor spoke the word.

"*Lahatsi!*" Mother Blessing shouted. She raised her hands as high as her bulk would allow and Kerry saw the energy ball that formed between them. Then Mother Blessing drew back and hurled it at Season.

Season didn't even speak, just flicked her wrist, almost casually, and the energy ball was diverted from its course. It hit a stand of cypress trees nearby and burst into flames, which sizzled and were extinguished in moments by the powerful rain. Watching the ease with which Season turned away what Kerry had believed to be a devastating attack, she realized with a shiver of fear that Season was the more skilled, the more potent, of the two combatants.

Which is bad, because Season has to die.

Not to mention that Kerry didn't want to be on the losing side of another fight to the death.

Season brought her hands together in a gesture that Kerry didn't know and then spread them quickly. A wave of power rippled the air, coming right toward them. Mother Blessing raised her hands in a warding gesture, and Kerry reflexively did the same. It worked;

the energy wave dissipated harmlessly around them.

Mother Blessing turned partially, glancing behind her to make sure Kerry was there. She took the stick and the gun from Kerry's hands, leaving her only the sword. "We'll need weapons," she said simply. "Use that, Kerry. Kill her."

"Me?" Kerry felt her stomach clench, her insides turn to liquid. She had never fought with a sword in her life. *But then,* she told herself, *there are a lot of things you've never done before. Doesn't mean you can't do them.* Half convinced by her own pep talk, she gripped the sword by its handle, holding it in both of her fists. To her astonishment, flames licked up and down the blade, as if gasoline had been spread on the steel and then ignited. Raindrops hissed on its fire as they struck it, evaporating instantly.

With the fire came new confidence— confidence she thought might have been magically instilled, but was good enough just the same. She pressed past Mother Blessing and went down the steps toward Season, fiery blade held out in front of her.

Season took a step back as Kerry approached, her eyes widening slightly, which added to Kerry's sensation of well-being. *This can work,* she realized. *She's genuinely worried that I can beat her.*

As she moved toward Season, she felt more sure of what to do, how to wield the flaming sword, as if the weapon itself were teaching her its technique. She advanced, blade flicking this way and that, weaving a web of light and flame. Season raised her right hand and manifested a similar weapon, a sword made from pure magical energy. She waved it around for a moment, as if gauging its heft, and it made a whistling noise as it cut through the air. Then she lunged suddenly toward Kerry, right leg thrown forward, left hand back, like a fencer. Kerry didn't even have to think—the fiery sword drew her hand across her body to parry the lunge, and Season's mystical blade slid harmlessly to Kerry's side.

Kerry moved easily from the parry to an attack, her own sword thrusting itself forward at Season, drawing her body into a straight line as it did. Season, her face all intense concentration now, blocked the thrust with a grunt of effort. The move threw her off balance, her feet slipping on the wet ground, and Kerry pressed her attack, twisting her blade around Season's and driving forward again. This time, the tip of it touched Season's leathers before the witch managed to bat it aside.

Season retreated two quick steps and raised her sword again. "This can only end badly for you," she warned through clenched teeth. "You don't know what you're in the middle of."

"The plan is for it to end badly for *you*," Kerry corrected. She stood her ground, feet planted, legs spread for stability. Every muscle that she had built up over the fall was functioning at peak performance. Mother Blessing had been right—she may not have been ready, but she was as ready as she'd ever be, and far more prepared than she had expected.

"Plans don't always work out the way they're supposed to," Season pointed out. "I would have thought you'd have learned that by now."

"You killed Daniel," Kerry reminded her, fury tightening her voice. "That's all I need to know."

"Like I said, you have no idea what you're

mixed up in, girl. If you back off now I'll try not to hurt you."

There was something in the witch's blue eyes that looked plaintive, even sympathetic. But Kerry was in no mood for it. She feinted to Season's left and then drove her sword, hard, toward Season's right. The witch parried, then drew her energy blade back and brought it forward again, slamming it into Kerry's with enough force to rip the flaming sword from her grasp. It spun twice in the air and splashed into swamp water, its flames dousing as it did.

All trace of sympathy gone from her face now, as if Kerry's resolve had steeled her own, Season charged in for the kill.

She lunged, the tip of her mystic blade slicing the air toward Kerry. Before it reached her, though, Kerry heard a sharp report from behind her, then another, and a third. Season's advance halted and she staggered back, blue eyes widening, mouth dropping open. Kerry whirled to see Mother Blessing sighting down the barrel of the rifle, which had a trail of smoke rising up from its opening. The woman fired again, the muzzle flash impossibly bright against the dark sky. Four spots appeared on

Season's black leathers, dark against dark, wet on wet.

Then Season bent forward at the waist, hands going up to her mouth. Kerry felt an unexpected sadness. She couldn't decide if it was because she hadn't been the one to finish Season off, or if it was something more than that, a kind of sorrow that the whole affair was ended. But ended it seemed to be.

Season had another surprise in store, though. She moved her hands a few inches away from her lips and spat four bullets into them, each one slick with her own blood. Holding them out before her, she smiled and dropped them to the ground. "You've got to do better than that," she said with a chuckle.

Mother Blessing hurled the weapon away, and raised the stick. "Not the gun and not the sword," she said, "but the rod will vanquish you."

Now Season's dry chuckle turned into a full-throated laugh. "That thing?" she asked. "Do you forget who gave you that, daughter?"

"Y'all are on my ground," Mother Blessing said sharply. "And Kerry is strong, stronger than she has any right to be. There'll be no walkin' away, not from this fight. Not this time." But Kerry noticed that in spite of the certainty of the words, the hand holding the old stick was shaking a little, and there was a quiver in the voice. She couldn't have imagined Mother Blessing being scared by anything, but there it was.

"I didn't come here to walk away," Season reminded her. "I came to make sure you don't. To make sure you aren't going to continue to haunt me for the rest of my days."

"I don't need to haunt what's dead," Mother Blessing said, her voice cracking even more. She held out the stick like it was a weapon and said, "*Manistera!*"

The stick crackled with energy, traces of blue lightning running up and down its length. After a moment, the energy lanced toward Season. But the witch deflected it with a quiet word and hastily upraised hands. Her magical sword was gone now, back to whatever place she had conjured it from.

Season clapped her hands together hard, creating a sound like a sonic boom. Kerry threw her hands over her ears too late. The boom echoed in them, and she had a feeling they'd ring for hours, if not days. But the blast of power that began at Season's clap and rippled out toward Mother Blessing like a stone in a pond was sliced by the older woman's rod. Where it passed, leaves and bark were torn from trees, mud upturned, water churned in the creek. Mother Blessing, Kerry, and the house seemed unaffected.

Season didn't release her hands, though. She kept them clasped together, and as long as she did, the wave continued. Kerry felt it pressing against her like a surging tide. Mother Blessing felt it too, she saw, and though she tried hard to hold onto her stick—*her rod,* Kerry mentally corrected—the force of Season's attack whittled away at it, bit by bit, until all that was left was the tiniest twig. As that happened, tears came to Mother Blessing's eyes—tears of rage or tears of sorrow, Kerry wasn't sure—and the older woman, who she had come to think of as all but invulnerable, was driven to her knees. The sight filled Kerry with terror more than anything else that had happened so far.

Finally, Mother Blessing threw the twig aside and brought her hands up in a "*Lashifoth!*" defense. Kerry joined in, shouting the word simultaneously with her and making the appropriate motions.

A golden glow engulfed them—the punishing rain actually bounced off its blurred edges—and Season's attack ceased. Still, Season didn't look particularly frightened or upset. "You didn't really think that stick would stop me, did you, daughter?" she asked. "A gift from me to you? Your first rod."

"I remember," Mother Blessing said, almost spitting the words. She crooked her finger at Kerry. "Help me up," she commanded.

Kerry wasn't sure she'd be able to budge the woman, but she hurried to comply. She didn't want Season to try anything more while Mother Blessing was on her knees.

"You're right," Season admitted then. "I am demonstrably more powerful than you, but on your home ground, and with your little helper, neither of us can get the upper hand. I had hoped to bring this little conflict to a close today, but apparently that's not to be."

Mother Blessing looked at Kerry, her eyes narrow, her mouth twisted into a scowl of utter hatred. "Don't let her go!"

Kerry already had her hands on Mother

Blessing's arms, trying to hoist the enormous woman to her feet. "What can I—?" she began.

Season interrupted her question. "Nothing. There's nothing you can do, child. Except perhaps ask the woman you call Mother Blessing to explain what happened here today. Make her tell you the *whole* story. The real story."

Kerry looked from one to the other— Mother Blessing, struggling to regain her footing, her face a mask of fury, and Season Howe, beautiful and calm even though her leather jacket still showed four bullet holes. As she watched, Season grew less distinct. Kerry thought at first that she was walking backward, getting lost in the still-pounding rain. But her legs weren't moving, and she wasn't getting smaller. She was just . . . *vanishing* was the only word that came to mind. Becoming less substantial. Kerry could see the trees behind her, through her, and the rain and the swamp, and then she was gone altogether.

Mother Blessing got a grip on Kerry's shoulders and forced herself to her feet. She looked at where Season had been a moment before, spat in that general direction, and stormed inside, slamming the door behind her. Kerry opened it again and walked in, wanting to talk to the woman, but Mother Blessing was already back on her scooter, wheeling toward her bedroom. When she reached it, she slammed that door, too.

And Kerry was alone with a million questions.

Kerry Profitt's diary, November 24.

There's something very wrong here. I can't ask Mother Blessing about it because (A) she hasn't come out of her room since the battle to end all battles that wasn't, and (B) because if what I think is true IS true, then she's been lying to me all along.

To me, and maybe to others.

See, the thing is, Season Howe addressed her as "daughter." Not once, but twice. I know, it could be some sort of traditional witchy form of address, indicating love and respect, but . . .

No, really. That was what I tried to convince myself she meant. Figure of speech, right? Problem there is that the rest of Season's speech seemed pretty precise—not one for flowery speeches, that witch.

And there's more. If Season gave Mother Blessing her first rod, that implies, at the very least, some sort of teacher-pupil relationship. Which could also be a mother-daughter relationship.

If Season is Mother Blessing's mother, then what else hasn't Mother Blessing told me? Or Daniel—because I'm sure if he knew Season was his grandmother, he'd have said something. Apparent age, among witches, doesn't mean much, as Mother Blessing herself told me. Mother Blessing looks older than Daniel and Season, but none of them look anywhere near their actual ages. So Season could easily be older than Mother Blessing.

I had a lot of questions before, but now I have . . . well, A LOT a lot. Like why was she so willing to send me to Las Vegas after Season, knowing that I had just barely begun my magical training? Was she testing me somehow? Testing my willingness to fight, my courage, my hatred of Season? Or maybe testing Season's strength? And having my van moved—sure, she let me find out about it, introduced me to Edgar. But why didn't she tell me when she did it, or even ask permission? My van, after all. And the biggie that's been haunting me is this—I've wondered how Mother Blessing could have described the destruction of Slocumb so well, when supposedly she was already on her way into hiding, trying to protect her unborn children. But what if the answer is that it wasn't Season who destroyed Slocumb, but Mother Blessing? That's a big stretch, I know. But it's one answer to something that's been gnawing at me. And it goes back to the fact that Mother Blessing has been hiding things, lying to me.

I hate that. Hate lies, hate liars. I had grown to respect Mother Blessing—she's a real character, and a bit of a handful, but she was teaching me a lot, and I was willing to use what she taught to help her further her goal. Since it was the same as my own goal—revenge for Daniel's murder.

If she's been dishonest with me this whole time, though, that changes things. It doesn't change the fact that Season killed Daniel (although it adds, like, this whole layer of almost Shakespearean irony to it, doesn't it? Mother persuades son to kill his grandmother, but grandmother turns the tables . . .). What it changes are all the whys, and some of the whos, if not the whats.

It also changes my plans. I wanted to stay here, to learn as much as I could from Mother Blessing, to try to get close to her since she is my only link now to Daniel—not that she's the easiest person to get to know, since she will almost never actually talk about herself. But now . . .

. . . now, I think I need to get away from here. Fast.

To paraphrase old Willie S., there's something rotten, but it ain't in Denmark. It's right here in the Great Dismal. And I have this feeling that the longer I sit in "my" room, typing on this laptop, the rottener it's getting. I think it'd be best to get myself gone before MB comes out of her room looking for me.

Is it because I've been thinking about Josh and his noir movies that the phrase "you know too much" comes to mind? Because whenever there's someone in those movies who knows too much, the person who says it is always trying to kill them.

I think maybe I know too much.

Guess it's time to go.

More later,

K.

End of Book Two

JEFF MARIOTTE is the author of more than fifteen previous novels, including several set in the universes of *Buffy the Vampire Slayer, Angel, Charmed,* and *Star Trek,* the original horror novel *The Slab,* and more comic books than he has time to count, some of which have been nominated for Stoker and International Horror Guild awards. With his wife, Maryelizabeth Hart, and partner, Terry Gilman, he co-owns Mysterious Galaxy, a bookstore specializing in science fiction, fantasy, mystery, and horror. He lives in San Diego, California with his family and pets, in a home filled with books, music, toys, and other examples of American pop culture. More information than you would ever want to know about him is at www.jeffmariotte.com.

**Read an excerpt from the second book
in the hot new series**

the

nine

lives

of

chloe

king

VOLUME TWO

The Stolen

by
CELIA THOMSON

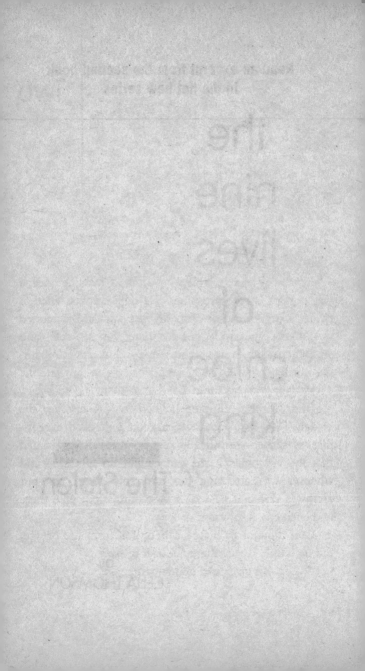

Two

"What do we do *now*?"

Paul bent over; there was a stitch in his side and he was puffing like an asthmatic. He only smoked once or twice a week—this was probably just plain old-fashioned out-of-shape-ness. He put his hand on his belly and straightened up. Amy was standing stiff as a rod, breathing normally, hands on her hips, glaring at him like the whole thing was his fault.

Behind them another helicopter was circling the bridge. They had been hovering like pissed-off dragonflies off and on since Friday night. Paul and Amy hoped that the National Guard had caught up to Chloe and whoever was attacking her and split them up—but almost a day had passed, and it didn't look like there had been any resolution.

Paul thought he'd seen a body fall from the bridge, but he didn't say anything about it to Amy.

"Well?" his girlfriend demanded again.

Paul sighed.

"I don't know—what do *you* think we should do?"

"Call her mom . . . ?" But even as she suggested it, Amy trailed off, knowing that it probably wasn't the right thing to do—or, more importantly, that it wasn't what Chloe would want. She ran her hands through her chestnut hair in exasperation, pulling on the roots. It was a leftover habit from when she was younger and tried to flatten her big, often frizzy hair every chance she got. "What do you think it was all about—*really*?"

They'd had this conversation several times in the last twenty-four hours, but somehow Amy was never satisfied with Paul's answers.

"I don't know. Drugs? Gangs? Some weird psycho game of tag?"

"Maybe it's got to do with her real parents or something. Maybe she's actually some sort of Russian Mafia princess."

Paul gave her a lopsided smile. Silently they started to walk home, not holding hands or anything. Like they had in the old days, when the three of them were just good friends. Before Chloe almost died from falling off Coit Tower. Before she and Amy got into that weird little snit they were in for days—and had just patched up. Before Chloe started seeing Alyec and Brian . . .

"You know," Paul said slowly, "a *lot* of weird shit has happened with Chloe in the last couple of months, don't you think?"

Amy shrugged. "Seems to me she got her period and turned into a total bitch. For a while, at least," she added hastily. Chloe might have been a bitch, but she was still Amy's best friend, and she was still missing.

"No, it's more than that." Paul frowned, crinkling his long white forehead. "I mean like her fall and the bruises on her face and her random absences from school—not to mention being totally incommunicado about general Chloe life issues."

"She was going to tell us everything," Amy remembered. "On the bridge . . . She was just about to explain *something.* . . ."

". . .when that freak with knives showed up." They looked at each other for a long moment.

"We were talking about her crush on *Alyec* when she jumped off Coit Tower," Amy suddenly pointed out.

"She didn't jump, she fell," Paul said, surprised at the way Amy said that. She was the only person on the planet who probably knew Chloe better than he did, and it was a really weird thing to say about their friend. At no point in her life, even at her gothiest moments, had Chloe *ever* seemed the suicidal sort. *A jackass, sometimes, but never suicidal.* Jumping up onto the ledge to get more attention had been a *little* rash, but they had been drinking, and it wasn't completely out of the range of typical Chloe behavior.

"Whatever," Amy said quickly, dismissing it. "Her life started going crazy after that. I'll bet it has something to do with him."

"That's insane. How could *thinking* about him have anything to do with getting mugged or whatever?" Paul asked. He tried not to laugh or smile but couldn't stop his dark eyes from twinkling. Fortunately Amy wasn't looking directly at him.

"No! Think about it." She began ticking off facts on the tips of her black glitter fingernails. "She was mugged right after we all split up at The Raven, then became a total hag when she started actually dating Alyec—and he's Russian, just like her. Maybe he's got her into something *bad.*"

"What about *Brian*, then?" Paul demanded. "As long as we're accusing random people of having somehow screwed up Chloe's life and sent assassins after her. Brian, the mysterious sort-of boyfriend who never kissed her, who isn't in school, and, most importantly— *who we've never seen?*"

Amy stared at him with blank blue eyes, at a loss for an answer. He was about to add a few more salient facts that proved she was a complete wacko with insubstantial—*crazy*—arguments, but then he noticed Amy's lips trembling and tears forming on her lower lids.

"She'll be okay. The National Guard is out there. We can call the police if you want or her mom later—let's say if we haven't heard from her in a few hours. Okay?"

Amy nodded miserably, and they continued walking home.

Three

Amy looked into the bottom of her locker hopefully. Nope, nothing. She was always making cute little notes for Paul and slipping them into *his* locker. Sometimes they were quick scrawls—*See you in English!*—and sometimes they were really intricate things she made the night before with cloth and her glue gun and stuff.

Not. Once. Had he ever done the same for her. She didn't want to outright *ask*—but how strongly did a girl have to hint? Now that she was finally dating a nice, nonpsycho boy, she figured she should cash in on some of the perks that were supposed to go along with it. She was being stupid, she knew, and selfish: Paul did all other kinds of nice boyfriendy things, like buying tickets ahead of time for movies they wanted to see and getting her a coffee at the café if she asked. And he would talk to her for *hours* on the phone about all sorts of things. . . .

But once, just once, Amy wished someone would treat her exactly the way she wanted them to. All that jazz about the Golden Rule and karma and stuff—her do-gooding didn't exactly seem like it was making its way back to her yet.

She closed the door dejectedly. Then she kicked it, hard enough to leave a dent with her steel-toed combat boots. Things were so up in the air and uncertain these days. Chloe was still gone. Amy cursed herself for not hearing the phone when she'd called; it had been jammed at the bottom of her backpack and she had been outside, looking for Chloe, of all people. Amy started checking her voice mail about a thousand times an hour, hoping to hear something from her friend, but nothing.

She was definitely worried about Chloe. No doubt about it.

But she also felt a little . . . left behind. It was like she had made the decision to go out with Paul and now all these strange and mysterious things were going on in Chloe's life that Amy *still* wasn't in on. . . .

Alyec's famous barking laugh echoed down the hall. Amy looked: he was slamming his locker closed and waving goodbye to his friends Keira and Halley—very non-Chloe friends—and balancing his flute case on top of his notebook. *Off for a music lesson.*

Amy realized this was her perfect opportunity to thoroughly interrogate the untrustworthy jerk. She snuck along twenty feet behind him, keeping her back to the lockers, Harriet the Spy style. She needn't have bothered, though: Alyec was too busy waving to people in the main corridor to notice her.

As soon as he turned down toward the music wing, Amy double-timed her tiptoeing until she was almost four feet behind him. She didn't have to do it *too* quickly, though: he was dragging one of his legs a little. *What is that, some kind of new cool-guy walk?*

She smoothed her big dark red hair back and put on her best frowny face. She wished she could do the cold-blue-eyed thing—she had the eyes for it, after all—but somewhere between her freckles and "aristocratic" nose, she tended to come across more goofy and pleasant than aloof.

"You could just, I don't know, talk to me like a normal person," Alyec said causally, without looking behind him.

After she got over her surprise, Amy was so angry at being caught out she almost stamped her foot.

"*Where's Chloe?!*" she demanded. "I swear to *God*, Alyec Ilychovich, if you fucking *hurt* her . . . !"

A couple of students toting big, cumbersome instrument cases turned the corner, giggling and holding sheet music.

Alyec easily scooped an arm around Amy and pulled her into an empty practice room. He put his hand over her mouth and held a finger to his own. He stood there, his ice blue eyes locked on her own blue ones, insisting that she stay quiet until the two other students had passed.

He watched out the door to see if anyone else was coming and then took his hand away from her mouth.

"If you're not going to talk to me normally," Alyec said with a faint smile, "at least don't go throwing a psycho fit about it in public."

The room was mostly dark, on an inside wing with no windows. It was small and cluttered with the sort of desks and chairs small groups of students would sit in while practicing. In just a few minutes some teacher would come in and flip on the lights and the next period would begin. But for now it was just the two of them, and they were very alone. Alyec's chiseled-perfect face was inches from Amy's.

"You . . . *jerk*!" Amy lifted up her foot to stamp on his toes. He very neatly spun her away so she was at arm's length.

"She is home sick today, that is all," he said patiently.

That was what all the teachers had said when Amy had asked them, too.

"I *know* she said she was safe, but I *saw* what happened on the bridge," Amy said, sticking out her chin.

Alyec's blue eyes widened, and for once he didn't have a comeback.

"What's all this about?" she demanded. "Why was someone trying to kill Chloe? Twice? You know. I *know* you know."

He opened his mouth, looking for something to say. "She really is just sick at home. With her mother," he repeated lamely.

There was a long, tense moment between them, Amy glaring at him, *daring* him to lie again. He finally looked away.

Amy slammed her fist up into his stomach.

"*Jerk!*" she said again, stamping out into the hallway as he leaned over, hand to his belly. She knew she couldn't have done any real damage with her small wrists and the "artist's hands" that Chloe always made fun of, but at least he looked surprised. Amy spun around.

"Chloe is my best. Friend. *Ever*," she hissed. "If anything happens to her because of you, I'm getting my cousin Steve to beat the living *shit* out of you—and anyone else you know!"

She turned and left, adrenaline—if not exactly triumph—ringing in her ears.

Four

Chloe was snoozing, *The History of the Mai* resting on her lap, its old leather cover making her sneeze occasionally in her sleep. This was her second time trying to get through the dense text since she'd arrived, and the second time it had put her promptly to sleep.

She was dreaming again. This time a cat as large as a person walked toward her quietly. Chloe waited for it to tell her something useful or do something. . . .

"Am I disturbing you?" it said.

Chloe jumped, finally awake. She was *not* dreaming. The weird and ghostly visage that had terrified her the night before was standing patiently before her. *That's just Kim; she's a freak,* Alyec had said.

And boy, was he right.

She was a skinny and oddly built girl, willowy and sleek. Her hair was shorter than Chloe's, shiny, full, and black—almost blue-black, almost Asian. She had high cheekbones.

And velvety black cat ears.

Big ones. The size they would be if a cat's head were blown up to human proportions.

Her eyes were an unreal green, slit like a cat's, completely alien and lacking the appearance of normal human emotion. She wore a normal black tunic-length sweater and black jeans. She was barefoot; her bony toes had claws at the end and little tufts of black fur. Chloe couldn't help thinking about hobbits, except the girl was drop-dead gorgeous. She seemed about Chloe's age, but it was hard to tell.

"Uh, no, I was supposed to be reading anyway," Chloe said, running a hand over her face, trying not to stare.

"I'm afraid I gave you a bit of a scare when you arrived. I'm sorry—I do not usually expect, new, ah, people to be wandering around late at night."

"Hey, uh, no problem. My bad." Chloe kept on trying to look elsewhere, not sure what to say, still trying not to stare.

"I am—"

"Kim, yeah, Alyec told me."

The other girl looked annoyed. "My name is *Kemet* or Kem, *not* Kim. No one calls me that, though, thanks to people like Alyec." She sighed, sinking gracefully into the chair next to Chloe. "*Kemet* means 'Egypt.' Where we are from originally, thousands of years ago."

Chloe made a note to ask her about that later, but something else intrigued her more.

"Is that your given name?"

"No." Kim stared at the floor. "My given name is Greska."

"Oh." Chloe tried not to smile.

"You can see why I wanted to change it."

"Absolutely."

There was a moment of silence. Kim was looking into Chloe's face as curiously as Chloe was trying to avoid staring at the other girl.

"So we're from Egypt originally?" Chloe asked, trying to break Kim's icy, blinkless gaze. She closed the book. "I . . . uh . . . hadn't even gotten that far."

"We're first recorded, or history first mentions us there: 'Beloved of Bastet and guarded by Sekhmet.'" Kim took the book up and flipped to a page with a map on it and an inscription in hieroglyphs. "We were created by her, according to legend."

Chloe didn't know where to begin with her questions—*Created by? Kim is my age and she can read ancient Egyptian writing?*

"Most of us in this pride are from Eastern Europe—"

"Wait, 'pride'?"

"Yes." The girl looked up at her coolly. If she'd had a tail, it would have been thumping impatiently. "That is the congregation our people travel in. Like lions."

"And Sergei is the leader of the . . . Pride?"

"No, just this one in California. There are four in the New World. Well, were. The one in the East is also primarily made up of Eastern European Mai." Kim flipped a few pages and showed another map with statistics and inscriptions, lines and arrows originating from Africa and pointing toward different places: migration routes to lower Africa, Europe, and farther east. "The pride in New Orleans tends to be made up of Mai who stayed in sub-Saharan Africa the longest. They like the heat," she added with a disapproving twitch of her nose.

"And the fourth one?"

"It was . . . lost," Kim said diffidently. "Anyway, we have been driven all over the world, away from our homes. Our pride managed to live in Abkhazia for several hundred years after we left the Middle East for good." She pointed to a little area shaded pink to the northwest of Russia, on the Black Sea. "The people there remained polytheistic long after the Roman Empire declined, Christianity swept the world, and Baghdad was destroyed by the Mongols."

"I get the feeling that there's a 'but' in here somewhere. . . ."

"Many Abkhazians were driven out in the middle of the nineteenth century to Turkey by domestic warfare with the Georgians. We got caught up in it and families separated, some staying, some fleeing, some going to the Ukraine or St. Petersburg. And then again, not so long ago, just when some started to move back and reunite with lost branches, there was new violence."

She put the book down and twitched her nose

again—more like a rabbit than a cat, Chloe decided. It seemed to signal a change in emotion.

"I'm an orphan, just like you," the girl continued bluntly. "My parents were killed or separated during the Georgian-inspired violence in 1988, before the Wall fell. They say I had . . . a sister . . . ," she said slowly, looking at Chloe with hope. "A year older than me. When I saw you come in, I thought we looked alike— and . . . maybe . . ."

Maybe a little, except for the ears, was Chloe's first, defensive reaction. If you took away the ears, they actually *did* look a little similar: dark hair, fair skin, light eyes, high cheekbones.

What if it were true? Chloe had *always* wanted a sibling, especially a sister; Amy was the closest she had, but it still wasn't quite the same, like someone you could whisper to in the middle of the night or talk about your crazy parents with. Someone who you could scream at when she borrowed your favorite piece of clothing without telling you and then brought it back reeking of cigarette smoke or just plain ruined.

Someone who could tell you it was okay when you suddenly grew claws.

So maybe she's a little freaky, but a sister is a sister. . . .

As many as 1 in 3 Americans
who have HIV... don't know it.

TAKE CONTROL.
KNOW YOUR STATUS.
GET TESTED.

To learn more about HIV testing,
or get a free guide to HIV and
other sexually transmitted diseases:

www.knowhivaids.org
1-866-344-KNOW

. . . A GIRL BORN
WITHOUT THE FEAR GENE

FEARLESS™

A SERIES BY
FRANCINE PASCAL

PUBLISHED BY SIMON & SCHUSTER

3029-01

BODY OF EVIDENCE
Thrillers starring Jenna Blake

"The first day at college, my professor dropped dead. The second day, I assisted at his autopsy. Let's hope I don't have to go through four years of this...."

When Jenna Blake starts her freshman year at Somerset University, it's an exciting time, filled with new faces and new challenges, not to mention parties and guys and...a job interview with the medical examiner that takes place in the middle of an autopsy! As Jenna starts her new job, she is drawn into a web of dangerous politics and deadly disease...a web that will bring her face-to-face with a pair of killers: one medical, and one all too human.

Body Bags
Thief of Hearts
Soul Survivor
Meets the Eye
Head Games
(with Rick Hautala)
Brain Trust
Last Breath

BY CHRISTOPHER GOLDEN

Bestselling coauthor of
Buffy the Vampire Slayer™: The Watcher's Guide

Published by Simon & Schuster